The Secret of the GOLDEN COWRIE

Gloria Repp

journey**forth**®

Greenville, South Carolina

The Secret of the Golden Cowrie

Edited by Suzette Jordan

Cover by Cheryl Weikel
Illustrations by Holly Hannon

© 1988 BJU Press
Greenville, South Carolina 29609
JourneyForth Books is a division of BJU Press.

Printed in the United States of America

ISBN 978-0-89084-459-5

20   19

Publisher's Note

Although Connie Lawrence lives in a godly home, she has been a Christian for only a few years, and she does not know the Lord or His Word very well. When she finds herself involved in a mystery surrounding the aunt she has come to love, she tries her best to make it turn out all right. The harder she tries, however, the more her plans seem to go awry. To make everything worse, Connie had hoped that solving this mystery would prove to herself and to Dan, her talented big brother, that she *could* do something well.

During this time, God brings several new friends into Connie's life: a wise and gifted young photographer; an unruly youngster and his pet raccoon; and the beloved Aunt Laura. God uses them and a pair of white swans to teach her about Himself. She begins to understand at last that He has a plan for her life and that He does answer prayer—in His own time and way.

Set in the wild and fascinating salt marshes of New Jersey, this is a story about waiting, about caring, and about the power of God's Word.

For Janelle,
who explored the marsh with me

For Jonathan and Andrew,
who washed so many dishes

Contents

Chapter One
A Prowler?

The first thing Connie Lawrence heard as she rushed into the house after school was Aunt Mabel's brisk voice. She stopped, peeked cautiously into the living room, and sighed with relief. Anything was better than Aunt Mabel in person.

But what was going on? Dad stood in the middle of the room, fidgeting with the book he held. Her mother was perched on the edge of the sofa, staring worriedly at the new speaker phone. They were both listening to Aunt Mabel.

"Laura will be coming home from the hospital on Friday. I'd like you to be there by then," Aunt Mabel was saying.

Who is Laura? wondered Connie.

"But Mabel," Mother began, "this is Thursday. I don't see how I can manage. . . ." She looked up at Connie's father with a helpless shrug.

Aunt Mabel went on firmly, "I wouldn't have bothered you, but I just can't get away for another two weeks. She's family, after all, so we have to do something."

She paused, and Connie knew she was shaking her grey head. "I'm afraid Laura's mind is slipping, though. She has this ridiculous idea that some prowler was in her house during the storm. Nobody pushed her down those steps—she just fell. Now don't you worry; when I get there, we'll see about a nursing home or something, but for now, I'll have to depend on you."

Connie's father spoke up. "Look, Mabel, you can't make her go to a nursing home if she doesn't want to."

"Don't tell me what I can do, young man." Aunt Mabel sounded grim, even over the phone. "I know what's best for Laura. She always has been flighty, and now it's beginning to get out of hand."

"Well, we can't possibly come before Saturday. We'll talk it over and call you back."

Connie edged into the room as her father switched off the phone, but neither parent seemed to notice her.

Mother sighed. "I can't think what to do. I've got the November bake sale at school next week." She pushed curly blonde hair away from her face. "Oh, and you're going out of town."

"Sounds like Mabel has found another life to organize," Connie's father observed wryly. "It's been years since we visited Cousin Laura. I wonder if she even wants us trooping over there to take care of her."

"She might be lonely now that her husband's died, especially since she has to stay in bed for a while. Maybe she won't mind," Mother said slowly. "From what Mabel said, though, she might be getting senile, and I wouldn't know what to do about that."

Connie took another step into the room, wondering if she was supposed to be listening to all of this. "What about me and Dan?" she asked. "Can we go too?"

Her mother gazed at Connie blankly, then turned to her husband. "That's going to be another problem, Ron."

"Can't they stay with somebody for those two weeks?"

"We don't know very many people yet, and it's such a long time," Mother said. "Well, maybe Dan could—the Trasks might not mind. But there's really no one I can leave Connie with. I guess she'll have to come."

Connie smothered a happy squeal and slipped through the doorway. Back in the living room, her mother was still fretting. "I'll have to phone the school about Connie—and the bake sale. Oh, and there's laundry to do, right away."

Mother's voice faded as Connie flew up the stairs to tell Dan. She burst into his room, forgetting to knock. "Hey, I'm going away on a trip with Mother for two weeks."

Her older brother looked up from his desk. "You're kidding."

"No, really." Connie settled herself on his neatly made bed. "Remember Aunt Mabel? She just phoned. I guess there's some cousin of Dad's who's been in the hospital and needs someone to take care of her until Aunt Mabel gets there." Connie felt a pang of sympathy for this unknown relative whose life Aunt Mabel was going to rearrange.

Dan put his pen down and leaned back in his chair, looking resigned. "Who is it?"

"They just called her 'Laura.' Do you know anything about her?"

"Yeah, Dad and I visited her a long time ago. I think you were too small to come along."

Connie leaned forward curiously. "What's she like? Where's she live?"

"She lives in New Jersey by the ocean. It's only a couple of hours drive from here, but it's like wilderness all around—there's a huge marsh and lots of woods. Her house is big and old-fashioned, the kind that Mother raves about."

He ran a hand through his blond hair. "I can't remember much about her, except that she was cross and gloomy most of the time."

"Is she a Christian?"

"Yes, it wasn't that; she was just a grumbling sort of person."

"I don't think Aunt Mabel likes her. Maybe that's why," Connie said slowly.

"Huh," Dan grunted. "Maybe she won't go along with what Aunt Mabel's got planned. That's enough to get anyone on Aunt Mabel's blacklist."

Connie nodded. She was still curious about Cousin Laura. Anyone that Aunt Mabel disliked couldn't be all that bad. She heard her mother's quick footsteps on the stairs and hurried out to ask what she should pack.

The trip sounded as if it were going to be exciting, even if this Laura turned out to be a grouch. Besides missing two weeks of school, there'd be the fun of living in a real old house, with all that wilderness to explore outside. And it might be nice not to have Dan around for a change.

At supper time, Connie could tell that her parents had agreed to Aunt Mabel's plan. Dad was doing his best to cheer Mother up.

"You'll love that old house she lives in," he told her. "And look at it this way: it'll be a wonderful chance to get some painting done. Connie can help you with the work, and then you can spend all afternoon painting out on the marsh. Think of it: geese flying into the golden sunset; a family of ducks dabbling in a grass-ringed pool; the solitary horizon of the sea. . . ."

Connie giggled. No wonder Dad was always getting asked to speak at conferences. He sure could be persuasive. Now Mother had an interested look on her face; she loved to paint outdoors. They started talking about arrangements for the trip, but Connie had stopped listening.

Dad's words gave wings to an idea she'd had since last week when her seventh-grade class had visited a photo exhibit at the art museum. What if she took her camera along on this trip? She'd try to get some really impressive pictures. Then she could enter them in the fine arts contest at school and have a chance at winning something for once. And maybe—maybe she'd even grow up to be a famous photographer.

Dan already knew that he wanted to be a scientist. Just last winter he'd spent all his savings on a telescope, and everyone had agreed that he'd make an excellent astronomer.

Connie helped herself to another carrot stick and chewed on it soberly. With a brother like Dan and a mother who was such a good artist, she sometimes felt like a . . . nothing. A nothing with plain brown hair.

Dan nudged her. "Stop dreaming, little sis, and pass the potatoes, will you?"

"I wish you'd quit calling me that," she said in her most dignified voice. She handed him the plate.

5

"Hey, you're probably going to be chief cook on this trip," he teased. "Oh, poor Laura, she'll never get well."

Connie tried to grin but sighed instead, remembering some of her cooking projects that had tasted so peculiar. Especially the one that Dan had named 'Carrot Flop.' Cooking sure wasn't her talent. Neither were painting or singing; she'd tried them too.

But photography will be different, she promised herself. And this trip will be my chance to get started.

The phone rang. Her mother left the table to answer it, murmuring, "That's Mrs. Trask, I hope." A minute later she returned, looking worried again. "Mrs. Trask said that they have some relatives visiting them, so they don't have room for you, Dan." She gave him an apprehensive glance. "I'll have to take you along."

"Oh, no," exclaimed Dan. "We're going to start a new section in science—I don't want to miss that. And then I'll have tons of work to make up."

Connie's parents exchanged glances. "Too bad I can't rearrange my schedule," her father said. For one hopeful moment Connie thought that something would happen so that Dan wouldn't have to come.

Then her mother shook her head. "I couldn't sleep at night if I left you alone in this house," she said to Dan. "I don't like your missing school, but it seems like this is the best thing to do. If only we hadn't just moved. . . ." Her voice trailed off sadly.

"Didn't Laura's husband have a large shell collection?" Dad asked in his let's-cheer-up voice. "I seem to remember your being fascinated by it the last time you were there, Dan."

"Yeah, I liked those shells," Dan admitted. He still looked gloomy.

"Hey, are you going to take your telescope?" Connie asked.

"Where?" He looked up from the circles he was drawing on his napkin. "Oh, there. Well, I guess so—that's not a bad idea. I could probably see a lot more, away from the lights of the city." He fell silent, and Connie could tell by the way he wolfed down the rest of the meal that he was thinking about some kind of project.

She tried to cheer her own self up. It might not be so bad having Dan along, especially if there was something strange going on at that old house. Connie glanced at her parents, still discussing the arrangements, and quickly finished her dessert. Was she the only one who remembered that Cousin Laura had complained about a prowler in her house? She wouldn't say anything about it, just in case she would not be allowed to come after all.

Chapter Two
The Wolf

Friday passed in a blurred rush of things to do at school and home: talks with teachers, planning, and packing. The time couldn't go fast enough to suit Connie, but finally Saturday morning arrived. She was jittery with delight as she helped to carry the suitcases out to the car. Dad would be driving the family to New Jersey and would stay long enough to get them settled, then return to Philadelphia.

At the beginning of the trip, Connie tried for a long while to concentrate on reading, but at last she gave up. She stared out the window, wondering what would happen in the next two weeks. As she jiggled excitedly on the car seat, Dan glanced at her over the edge of his book. "Can't you keep still?" he said.

She slid closer to him. "What does 'senile' mean?" she asked in a low voice. "Mother said that Aunt Mabel seems to think this Laura person is going senile."

"We're supposed to call her 'Aunt Laura,'" he reminded her. Then he considered the question. "When people get senile, sometimes their brain doesn't work the way it should. They forget things a lot or act a little strange."

"You mean she might be crazy?" asked Connie in fascination.

"Well, not really crazy," Dan told her, "and just because Aunt Mabel said it—"

"Yeah, I know." Connie remembered that Aunt Mabel didn't really approve of her, either. 'So bouncy,' Connie had heard her say once. 'Flighty, too. You'll have trouble with that one.'

Flighty? Connie had looked up the word in the dictionary, curious to see what Aunt Mabel thought of her. Then she wished she hadn't. "Subject to flights of fancy," it had said, "not stable: IRRESPONSIBLE; also: SILLY."

Come to think of it, that was the word Aunt Mabel had used to describe Cousin Laura. *Flighty.* She hugged the word to herself, already feeling a link with her new-found relative.

But when would they get there? Connie sighed with impatience and turned to look out the window for the hundredth time.

During the trip they had passed long stretches of flat farmland and countless small towns, all winter-dreary and dull under the gray sky. Now the road wound through tall pine trees that looked dark and mysterious in the fading afternoon light. Was this the kind of wilderness that Aunt Laura lived in?

Connie leaned forward. "Dad, are we almost there?"

"It won't be long now," he assured her. "See the sign?" He waved a hand at one of the brown signs that Connie had already noticed along the way. It had an arrow pointing in the direction they were going, with the words *National Wildlife Refuge* above the tan silhouette of a flying goose. "Laura lives right next to the refuge," he explained.

There was no time for Connie to ask about the refuge, for now they were turning off the road to climb a steep driveway. Through leafless trees, Connie caught sight of the house.

It was tall and white, with high pointed gables and four little dormers perched like eyebrows above them. There would be many rooms inside it, Connie thought, and maybe an attic that was dark and dusty, filled with secrets.

"Heh, heh, heh . . ."

In spite of herself, Connie jumped. Dan must have seen the look on her face; he was laughing his spooky laugh. The way he did it always made her arms get goose bumps.

"Oh, stop—" she scolded him, not taking her eyes from the house.

"What a wonderful old place," her mother exclaimed. In Philadelphia there were lots of old houses, and her mother was always admiring them, although Connie had never been sure she'd like to actually live in one.

But Dad had parked beside a small garage at the end of the driveway, and now everyone was getting out. As Connie followed her brother down the cobblestone walk, the front door swung open.

A dark-haired woman stood there, watching them as they approached the house. In a toneless voice she remarked, "You must be Laura's relatives."

"Yes," Connie's father answered quickly. "Are you Mrs. Atkins?"

"That's right." She examined them silently for a long minute and then stepped back so they could enter the dim hallway.

"We certainly appreciate your taking care of Laura." Connie's father smiled down into the woman's long, lean face.

"Well, I try to minister any way that I can," Mrs. Atkins told them. "My ministry is with the sick and the poor. I cook and I clean and I try to make them comfortable. It don't pay much, but I know I'm earning some stars in glory, by and by."

Connie fidgeted under the woman's serious gaze.

Mrs. Atkins went on, "Laura's bedroom is over here." She started to leave, then stopped. "Mind you, Laura Hendrick is not an easy patient. You make sure she stays down, just like the doctor said. And don't let her worry about things."

Briskly she led them from the hall into a long, shadowy room. Connie noticed the stone fireplace against one wall and guessed that this was the living room. Mrs. Atkins opened a door off the living room, saying, "She's right in here, waiting for you."

Connie peered eagerly past her father into the bedroom. Its two pink lamps shone on a small, silver-haired woman who was propped up in bed. Her plump face beamed a welcome that crinkled the corners of her blue eyes.

"Barbara and Steve!" she exclaimed in a musical voice. "It's so good to see you." She waved them closer.

Then she smiled at Connie's brother. "I remember you, Dan. Are you still doing scientific projects?" At his shy nod, Aunt Laura's bright gaze turned to Connie, who suddenly felt anxious for her approval.

"And you must be Connie." The smile lines around her eyes deepened. "I'm glad you came too." She looked as if she might have said more, but Mrs. Atkins put her head back into the bedroom.

"Laura, I'll be going now, but I'll stop by in a few days to see how you're getting along. And don't you fret about any more strange goings-on. Just keep the doors and windows locked."

Connie saw her parents exchange worried glances. Mrs. Atkins turned her gaze to Connie's mother. "Supper is in the oven and everything's ready upstairs. Laura has already eaten. You'd better let her alone now."

Connie's mother began to say something, but the woman had gone. They heard the quick tap of footsteps across the living room floor and then a click as the front door was pulled shut.

Aunt Laura leaned back against the pillows and laughed. It was a rich, bubbling laugh that made Connie want to join in without knowing why. Shaking her head, the little woman exclaimed, "Oh, the very goodness of the good! Sometimes it can be a little tiresome."

Still smiling, she gave Connie's mother a searching glance. "And now Mabel has sent you here, presumably to keep me in order until she can take over. Barbara, I do hope that you don't consider me your ministry too."

To Connie's surprise, her mother laughed. "I'm afraid you're going to find out that I'm not nearly as capable as your Mrs. Atkins."

Aunt Laura nodded, and a dimple showed in her cheek. "Yes; then we'll get along fine."

A spasm of pain crossed her face, and she frowned for an instant. Then she took a deep breath and added faintly, "I think I'll rest for a bit. I'm sorry I can't be up to welcome you properly."

"We'll manage," Connie's father assured her. "You get some sleep."

In the kitchen they found that the table was already set and a casserole was warming in the oven. Mrs. Atkins had left them a note with a sketch that showed where each person was to sleep.

"Mrs. Atkins must be the lady from Laura's church that Mabel talked about hiring until we got here. She's not very friendly, but she certainly is efficient," Mother said.

She was poking through the contents of the refrigerator. "Look, here's a salad too." She took the plastic wrap off the salad bowl and sighed. "I don't think she approved of me. I hope I can handle all of this."

Dad put his arm around her. "Sounds like Laura doesn't need quite as much efficiency as she's been getting. You'll do fine."

After they had eaten, Dad jumped up from the table, still looking determinedly cheerful. "Okay, kids, let's bring the suitcases in so I can get your mother settled before I have to leave."

The sketch showed that Connie's room was at the near end of the second floor, with Dan's right across the hall from her. The long hall seemed dark and gloomy, but as soon as Connie stepped into her bedroom, she knew she was going to like living here.

The lamp was on, casting a circle of light on pale green wallpaper that was sprinkled with tiny yellow roses. A bright yellow quilt covered the bed, and long green draperies shut out the dreary winter evening. On the bedside table she found an old-fashioned pitcher filled with pine sprigs and feathery plumes of dried grass.

Now who would have thought of this? she wondered, lightly touching the prickly pine needles. Somehow it didn't seem like the kind of thing that Mrs. Atkins would do. Aunt Laura might, but she couldn't walk up the stairs. Connie sniffed happily at the scent of pine and kicked off her shoes.

The floor was made of polished wood, but a soft green rug lay beside the bed, and it felt good to scrunch her toes into it. She dropped her coat onto a cushioned, green rocking chair and ran across the hall to see how Dan was doing.

"Hey, I love my room," she exclaimed. "I can't wait for Mother to see it."

Dan was already setting up his books on a desk in the corner, and he glanced absent-mindedly over one shoulder. "It's late, kid, and Mother's probably got her hands full right now. Don't you think you'd better get to bed?"

"I guess so," Connie said reluctantly. She had wanted to ask Dan if he knew anything about the 'strange goings-on' that Mrs. Atkins had mentioned.

As she left his room, she saw her mother coming up the stairs. "Hi, honey. Did you find your room all right?" she asked.

"Yes, it's really pretty." Connie pushed the door wide open, and her mother glanced inside.

"It does look nice," she agreed. She gave Connie a hug. "Time for bed now. I'll see you in the morning."

But Connie clung to her for a moment longer. "Does Aunt Laura act like she's senile?" she whispered.

Her mother gave her a startled glance, then shook her head. "No, not so far," she whispered back. "But don't you worry about it."

Connie nodded. Aunt Laura had seemed quite normal to her too. Satisfied, she said, "Okay then, good night."

She changed into her nightie and decided to open a window at the side of the room. She pushed aside the draperies to see what kind of window was there and discovered a whole row of windows and a door that led to a balcony.

Intrigued, she put on a coat over her nightie and stepped out into the cool night. The balcony on which she stood seemed to run the whole length of the house. At first, all she could see beyond its edge was darkness. Then she made out the black shadows of trees to her left, and in the distance before her, a pale sweep of mist that might be the sea. In the stillness she could hear a faint dripping of moisture from the trees.

As she stood at the railing, the shadowy darkness seemed to shift, to rearrange itself, as if something were passing through. She waited, straining her eyes into the night.

Now she could see it: a moving shadow on the back lawn that became a big, rough-coated animal. It padded silently past, paused to look over its shoulder at the house, then slipped between the tree trunks and was gone.

Connie took a deep, shivering breath. She'd never heard of wolves in New Jersey, but that certainly looked like one. The night felt chilly all of a sudden, and she stepped back into the warm haven of her room.

Remembering Mrs. Atkins's warning, she locked the door behind her and pulled the draperies tightly shut.

She yawned, wishing that she'd already brushed her teeth, and headed for the bathroom. On her way back, she noticed that the light was still on in Dan's room. She gazed curiously down the length of the hall. There were at least two bedrooms between her room and Mother's, which was all the way at the end. What might be in those rooms?

She tiptoed down the hall and cautiously tried the doorknob of each one. Yes, they were locked, just as she'd guessed.

She scrambled back to her own room and crawled into bed, still thinking about those locked doors. An old house like this might be hiding something interesting, she told herself sleepily. The thought gave her a delicious sense of mystery, and she snuggled contentedly into the soft feather pillow.

The next morning while they were sitting over a late breakfast, Mother told Connie and Dan that instead of going to church and leaving Aunt Laura alone, they would all listen to a sermon tape that Mrs. Atkins had left. It sounded like a good idea to Connie. She'd been afraid that Mother would insist on sending them off to a strange church with someone like Mrs. Atkins.

Mother set up the tape player in Aunt Laura's bedroom, and they each picked out a chair. As Connie listened, she studied Aunt Laura, who lay with her eyes closed, a look of concentration on her face.

Aunt Laura hadn't come to the kitchen for breakfast; apparently she wasn't allowed to get out of bed. But she had called both Dan and Connie into her room and had talked to them, looking pretty in her pink bed jacket. Connie had brought her a breakfast tray, and Aunt Laura had handled it deftly, although she hadn't eaten much.

I've watched her all morning, Connie thought, and she doesn't seem to be the least bit senile. She's really sort of nice. Why did Dan remember her as being cross and gloomy?

The tape had just ended when they heard someone pounding on the front door. Mother ran to open it.

Chapter Three
The Lookout Tree

"Well, hello there," boomed a deep voice. "Who is this lovely lady with the golden hair? No, don't tell me! You're Laura's cousin, come to take care of her. And I'm Ben Stafford."

Connie heard Mother say faintly, "Won't you come in?"

But the short, stocky man was already in, striding into Aunt Laura's bedroom. He was dressed in the plaid shirt and dark pants of an outdoorsman and had spiky white hair. He wore big green fishing boots, half-laced.

His pink face creased into a smile. "Well now, Laura, you're looking fine this morning. Just fine. You've got roses in your cheeks." His deep voice was smooth, almost slippery-sounding, Connie thought, and it was too loud. Did he think Aunt Laura was deaf?

"Is this your wonderful family?" He turned to survey the group, and for a moment Connie thought he was going to bow, but he didn't.

"Yes, Ben." With a visible effort, Aunt Laura sat up straighter in bed. "This is Barbara Lawrence—and Dan and Connie."

To them she explained, "Mr. Stafford has been keeping an eye on things for me; he's a very kind neighbor."

"Oh, it's nothing at all, nothing at all." Mr. Stafford waved his hand. "Just glad to help anytime. Anytime." He eased into a chair and lowered his voice. "Wanted to make sure everything's still all right with you folks. Didn't see any strangers around here last night, did you?"

"I don't think so," Aunt Laura said calmly.

"Why?" asked Mother in a worried voice. Connie leaned forward to listen.

"I heard there was a burglary not too far from here. Not far at all—last night," Mr. Stafford said. "Just made me wonder about you. Just wondered." He jumped up and sent a smile around the room. "Well, I'll get going. Got me a cake in the oven, and I can't take a chance on it burning."

He clumped out of the room in his big boots, calling back, "Now Laura, I'll check in later. Don't hesitate to ask—anytime. Anytime."

"Thank you, Ben," Aunt Laura said softly. As soon as he had banged out the front door, she sank back against the pillows with a sigh. "He means so well, that man, but he is totally exhausting."

She closed her eyes for a moment and then opened them to smile at Connie and Dan. "Have you had a chance to explore outside yet? There might be a pair of swans down in the marsh. Dan, I think you'll like our lookout tree over in Deer Meadow."

Before either of them could answer, Mother interposed, "That's a good idea. And Laura, you need to rest for a while. Come on, kids." Connie and Dan followed her from the room.

After she had closed Aunt Laura's door, Mother said, "I'd like you two to finish unpacking—right now."

"Okay." Connie agreed hurriedly, before Mother could think of anything else for them to do. "Hey, Dan, I'm going to beat you."

"Huh," he grunted. But he followed close behind as she ran up the stairs, and while she worked in her room, she could hear him moving around pretty fast. He was ready by the time she had finished putting her things away. At the last minute she remembered to grab her camera, and they left together by the front door.

As they walked around to the back of the big white house, Connie saw the balcony she'd discovered outside her room last night. Each of the rooms next to hers seemed to have its own door to the balcony, too. She stopped to take a picture that showed her balcony door, then ran to catch up with Dan, who had walked to the edge of the back lawn.

"We could go down to the marsh and look for some swans," she suggested hopefully.

But Dan was staring into the woods. "I'd like to find that lookout tree," he said. "There's a path around here somewhere that goes back to Deer Meadow. Maybe this is it." He ducked into a stand of pine trees that grew close by the side of the house.

They looked like very old trees to Connie, and their thin, dark trunks rose straight and bare to a great height. When she tilted her head back, she could see that each one held up an umbrella of green needles, far at the top.

She followed as Dan led the way down a narrow path that felt soft and springy under her feet. It wound between the pines, which stood close together in orderly rows, like soldiers.

The path branched, and the left fork took them to the edge of a broad field that was ringed with woods. "I think they call this Deer Meadow because sometimes the deer come here to feed," Dan explained.

"Did you ever see any?"

"Yes, once. Here, let's cut across this way." He stepped across a sprawling wire fence and followed it around the edge of the meadow.

Connie paused in front of a weathered, grey fence post and snapped a picture of the small birdhouse nailed to it. "Look—it's so cute with the little round hole for a door. Anybody home?" she asked, peering inside. "Nope, I guess they've all gone for the winter."

"Aunt Laura's husband was crazy about bird watching," Dan commented. He stopped to look around the field. "See, he's got those things all over. They're nesting boxes, actually."

"He died, didn't he?" asked Connie. "I wonder what happened."

"I heard Dad say that he took his boat out and got caught in a bad storm—last March, I think it was."

"So he drowned," Connie said. She thought sympathetically about Aunt Laura, who must have waited and waited for him to come back.

"Dan," she said suddenly. "She's not like you remembered, is she?"

He had been studying the far side of the meadow, and he gave her a puzzled look. "Who?"

"Aunt Laura. What do you think of her?"

"Well, she sure doesn't act senile, for one thing."
Slowly he added, "Besides that, I think she's different
now. She never used to smile so much."

"I wonder why," Connie mused.

"I don't know." Dan took a sudden step forward. "Hey,
maybe that's their lookout tree." He started off at a trot
toward the far end of the field, where a lone pine tree
towered majestically over the surrounding woods.

Connie followed. A ladder had been nailed to the
side of the tree, and she stopped to take a picture of
it. By the time she caught up with him, Dan had climbed
the ladder to a narrow, railed platform high up in the
tree.

"Hey, this is great." He peered down at her. "Come
on up."

She was already halfway up the ladder. There was
plenty of room for them both, and she crouched next
to Dan on the rough planks of the platform.

"Over there's the salt marsh." He pointed off to their
right, where ribbons of grass crisscrossed wide pools
of glistening water that seemed to stretch all the way
to the horizon.

"Oh, it's beautiful!" exclaimed Connie. "It's so big!"

"Part of it belongs to the bird refuge. There's a path
that goes right down into it." Dan got to his feet. "Let's
look around a little more, and then we'd better head
back. It must be lunch time. I'm starved."

But Connie had caught a flicker of movement down
in the marsh. "Wait—there's someone—" She shaded
her eyes so she could see better. A tall black woman,
dressed in green, was walking briskly through the grass.
She was carrying something that might be a camera.

In another minute she had disappeared into the trees at the edge of the marsh.

"I wonder who that was," said Connie.

"Lots of people come to the refuge," Dan said. "Let's get going."

When they reached the pine woods, Connie remembered the wolf she had seen go in there last night. She slowed down to look for tracks and then realized that they wouldn't show up on the thick layer of pine needles.

Maybe she hadn't really seen it, anyway. Dan was always saying that she had an imagination that worked overtime. She'd better make sure it was a wolf before she told anyone. Perhaps she could get a picture of it.

During the afternoon, while Connie finished arranging things in her bedroom, she thought about the work her teacher had assigned. The math pages were the worst. Since she always had trouble with math, she was supposed to do one page every day. Besides that, the teacher had told her to keep a record, called a journal, of all the interesting things she saw or did. If she made a collection of some kind, it would count for extra points.

Except for the math, the assignment sounded like more fun than going to school. Connie took out the looseleaf notebook that would be her journal. She wouldn't do any homework today, but she did want to tell about the Lookout Tree. She nibbled on the end of her pencil for a moment, thinking about it, and then began to write.

That evening, after listening to another sermon, they sang hymns together while Dan accompanied them on the piano that was in the living room. Aunt Laura joined in with her deep alto voice, watching through the open door of her bedroom. "My, he certainly does play well," she remarked.

Connie wondered, as she always did when she heard Dan play, if she would *ever* sound like that. "I wish I could be good at something—really good," she told herself for the hundredth time.

Well, maybe it would be photography. She'd taken a lot of pictures today. A real photographer would carry around a little notebook, though, and write down each picture he took. That's what she should do. Mother asked Dan to play a Chopin prelude, and when he began, Connie slipped upstairs. She'd start on her picture notebook. Anyhow, it was a good way to avoid the possibility of having to play one of her dumb little songs.

She was all ready for bed and had even turned out her light when she decided to take a look outside for the wolf. Perhaps if she waited long enough, she would catch another glimpse of him. She put on her coat, slipped out onto the balcony, and curled up in a small white chair that stood back from the railing.

Tonight there were no clouds covering the sky, and it was radiant with stars. Carefully she examined the dark mass of woods beside the house and, seeing nothing there, gazed dreamily in the direction of the marsh. The wind blew through the pines with a soft rushing murmur that rose and fell, making her sleepy.

During a lull in the wind's song, she heard something rustle. Wide awake, she jerked toward the pine trees. What was walking around in there?

She sat very still, trying to make out the difference between the shadows that were tree trunks and the blackness of the woods. "It must have been the wolf," she told herself, and she tried not to think about the burglary that Mr. Stafford had reported. But last night . . . the wolf hadn't made any noise.

The busy putt-putt-putt of a small car broke into her thoughts. It came closer and closer, finally stopping nearby—perhaps in the driveway on the other side of the house. Aunt Laura must be having a late visitor.

She stayed where she was for a while longer, staring into the darkness until her eyes grew heavy. Yawning, she stood up at last to go inside. A light flicked on in the room that was two doors down from hers, and she stopped to stare at it curiously. Was someone using that bedroom?

With cold-stiffened fingers she fumbled for the doorknob of her own door. Maybe tomorrow she could find out.

Chapter Four
Discovering Stella

When Connie opened her curtains the next morning, she could see the sparkling marsh from her window. During breakfast she told Dan, "I've got to go down and see what the marsh is like. I just can't wait any longer."

"Hope you're not disappointed," he said briefly, and heaped another spoonful of jelly on his toast.

"Why don't you come too?" she suggested.

He shook his head. "Got a lot of assignments to do," he mumbled through a mouthful of toast. "Don't want to get behind. This is Monday, remember."

"That's right," Mother said. "Connie, I think you had better do your math and some piano practice before you go anywhere."

"Okay," said Connie, but she glanced longingly out the kitchen window. Something green caught her eye. It was a Volkswagen beetle, parked behind the garage. Was that the car she'd heard last night?

"And before you start on that," Mother added, "would you take Aunt Laura's breakfast to her? Carry in the tray first; then come back for her cocoa."

Aunt Laura was sitting up, reading by the light of her bedside lamp. She held the book close to her eyes, as if she couldn't see it very well. Connie tried to make her voice cheerful and brisk, the way she imagined a good nurse would sound.

"Good morning! Are you ready for some breakfast?"

"Well, thank you, Connie." Aunt Laura smiled at her and took off her glasses. She had young-looking, very blue eyes. After Connie had settled the tray on the bed, she thought how dark the small room was, compared to the bright day outside.

"I'll open your curtains if you like," she offered.

"That's a good idea," Aunt Laura agreed. "This used to be my sewing room, and I always sat by the window so I could look out."

As Connie pulled open the flowered curtains, she noticed a pair of tall glass bottles on the window sill, and she was careful not to knock them over. One was rosy pink, the other pale green, and the morning light made their colors glow. She took another quick glance toward the marsh, but down here at ground level, she could see only trees.

"Connie, don't forget the cocoa," called her mother from the kitchen.

"Oh, yes." Connie dashed back to the kitchen.

"Here, and be careful," warned her mother. She handed Connie a pink china pitcher that steamed with the delicious aroma of chocolate. Gingerly, half-afraid that she would drop it, Connie carried the pitcher to Aunt Laura's bedside.

"M-mm, that smells wonderful." Aunt Laura leaned forward to pour herself a cup of cocoa and asked, "Do you like cocoa?"

"Yes," Connie said, surprised that she would care.

"Then why don't you stay and have some with me?" Connie hurried to get herself a cup, and then she pulled a small green armchair up close to Aunt Laura's bed. After Aunt Laura had filled her cup, she sipped at it happily. "I'm the only one in my family who likes cocoa," she confided. "So I never get to have it."

Aunt Laura chuckled. "It's my absolute favorite— my husband always teased me about it. He said I never grew up, because I'd rather have cocoa than coffee."

She took a sip from her cup and fell silent. She seemed to be gazing through the window at the trees outside, and Connie found that she felt comfortable just sharing the bright morning together.

The stillness was broken by the sound of a car starting up close by. Connie recognized the putt-putt-putt of a Volkswagen beetle. It must be the green one she had seen in the driveway.

"Sounds like she's up early again," Aunt Laura murmured. Connie must have looked puzzled, for Aunt Laura smiled and said, "I guess you don't know about Stella."

"Did she come in last night?" guessed Connie.

Aunt Laura nodded. "Actually, she got back yesterday afternoon. She must have gone out to church last night. Stella's been away at a conference over the weekend—that's why you haven't met her yet."

"Is she living with you?" Connie asked in confusion.

"Just visiting. I told your parents about her, but I don't think Mabel knows. She wouldn't approve."

Aunt Laura gave Connie a wry smile and went on. "Stella is the daughter of a dear friend of mine. She travels around quite a bit, because she does research projects for an organization—I can't remember the name—it's something scientific and rather complicated."

That didn't sound very interesting, but Connie asked, "What kinds of things does she study?"

"Let's see," Aunt Laura mused. "I know she writes articles about wildlife, and she does quite a bit of photography."

Connie leaned forward, suddenly alert. "She's a photographer?"

"Yes, an excellent one. There are several magazines that publish her work."

"Will she be here for lunch?" asked Connie hopefully.

"Probably not. She keeps to herself quite a bit and usually gets her own meals, so you might not see much of her. In fact, she often spends the whole day out in the salt marsh. I think she even forgets to eat."

Connie nodded, understanding. Mother was like that sometimes about her painting.

Aunt Laura continued, "I had told Stella's mother about our wonderful wildlife refuge that's so close by, and last August Stella wrote to ask if she could come here to do some work on a project." She wiped her small hands daintily on a napkin and leaned back against the pillows. "I hope you'll have a chance to talk to Stella; I admire her tremendously."

She closed her eyes, and Connie decided that it was time to leave. She stood up and gathered the breakfast things together. Aunt Laura murmured, "It's nice to have you here, Connie. We'll have to do this again."

Connie slipped quietly from the room and spent the next half-hour helping her mother in the kitchen. While she worked, she thought about what she had learned. Stella must be the black woman she had seen down in the marsh. It had looked as if she carried a camera. It was exciting to think that here was a real photographer—maybe she could get to know her.

"I'm going to help Aunt Laura with her bath now," her mother said. "Why don't you work on your math here in the kitchen so you'll be close by in case I need anything." She smiled sympathetically. "I know you want to go outside, but do a good job on that math."

A few minutes later when the phone rang in the quiet kitchen, it startled Connie. She jumped up to answer it. A man's voice asked, "Is Mr. Hendrick there, please?"

"No, he isn't," Connie began.

She started to explain about Aunt Laura's husband, but the voice went on, "This is Jason Ross of Trans World Maritime Museum. We had corresponded with Mr. Hendrick about one of his cowrie shells, and I was wondering why we haven't heard from him. Perhaps you could help us, Mrs. Hendrick?"

"But I'm not Mrs. Hendrick," Connie said hastily. "Mr. Hendrick died. And I don't know anything about a shell. His wife can't come to the phone right now, but—"

"Oh, I'm sorry to hear that," said the man politely. "I will call back later when it's more convenient." He hung up before Connie could say anything more.

She scribbled a reminder about the phone call on a corner of her math paper and impatiently tackled another row of problems. These long division things seemed to be taking forever.

It wasn't until after lunch that Connie finally had a chance to get out of the house. Dan had told her to take the wide path that crossed the back lawn. It would lead her beside the marsh, and she wouldn't get lost if she stayed on it.

"What makes him think that I'm going to get lost right away?" she asked herself. She took a deep breath of the cool air. It smelled salty, like the sea, and she quickened her pace.

The path sloped upward through leafless, brown-limbed trees, and before long she found herself at the top of a sandy bluff. She stepped to the edge and exclaimed in delight. Below her lay the marsh. It was an immense, watery wilderness that seemed to stretch for miles, bounded only by the wide-arched blue sky and the distant horizon. Gazing at the broad expanse, she felt her spirit lift with an unexpected sense of freedom.

A low, gabbling murmur—the sound of birds—filled the air, but she couldn't see any of them from here. She left the path, weaving her way between stunted evergreens and hummocks of marsh grass, and hurried down the sandy slope so she could get closer to the water. A pair of geese with long black necks looked up at her from the nearest pond. She skidded to a halt and stood quietly, admiring their handsome bronze plumage.

After a minute the geese paddled to the far end of the pond and began dipping for water plants. Connie followed them along the shore. As she rounded a clump of cedar trees, her eyes still on the geese, she almost ran into someone who stood there holding a camera.

"Oh, I'm sorry!" she exclaimed. She glanced at the camera and recognized the black woman. "You must be Stella. Are you taking pictures of the geese? What kind are they?"

She scolded herself silently for babbling like a little kid, but Stella didn't seem to mind. "Hi, Connie, I've been wanting to meet you," she said with a smile. She was tall and slim, and right away Connie noticed the earrings she wore: dangling gold ones that were shaped like tiny pine cones.

Stella raised her camera. "They're Canada geese," she said softly. She focused for a long moment, then snapped the picture. Connie suddenly remembered her own camera and took a picture too.

"Aunt Laura said you're working on a research project. Are you getting photographs for it?" she asked eagerly. Stella nodded, writing something in the notebook she carried, and Connie wished she had remembered to bring hers.

Stella closed the notebook. "I'm doing a study on some of the migratory birds," she explained. "It's especially interesting how they make use of bird refuges." With Connie beside her, she walked slowly along the sandy margin of the pond. "This refuge has some Canada geese that stay here all year round, but there are other flocks that just stop for rest and food on their way farther south."

As they passed a tangle of briars, Connie saw a heap of black feathers on the ground. She stepped over to look at them.

"Oh, what a shame," exclaimed Stella, joining her. "It looks as if some animal caught a black duck."

Connie picked up one of the glossy black feathers and stroked it. "Poor thing."

"Here's a pretty one." Stella handed her a tiny white feather that was tipped with orange.

"Thank you. Oh, it's so soft and downy." Connie made up her mind as she spoke. "I'll keep these. I'm going to collect feathers for a school project."

"Good idea." Stella was studying the muddy ground. "The scoundrel left some tracks."

Connie bent over them with her. "It must have been the wolf." She glanced shyly at Stella. "I think I saw a wolf the other night."

"Hmm." Stella followed the line of tracks to where they wandered along the edge of the pond. "A wolf usually walks in a fairly straight line. This fellow has what they call staggered prints: see how they go this way, then that way? He drags his toes, too. I think it might have been a dog—a pretty big one."

"How did you learn all that?" Connie asked admiringly.

Stella laughed. "From Sam—he's my oldest brother and the best friend I ever had. He taught me an awful lot. I used to think he knew everything in the whole world."

She smiled at Connie and turned from the water's edge. "Have a good time exploring. I think I'd better get back to the house now and do some writing."

Connie watched her stride away through the marsh grass with her camera looped over one shoulder and her earrings swinging jauntily.

Maybe if I come down to the marsh a lot, I'll get to know Stella better, she thought. That was something to look forward to.

For several minutes more she strolled along a twisting, muddy path. She paused to watch another pair of Canada geese and caught sight of a fisherman farther on, where the path took a turn out toward the water.

He wasn't fishing; he was just sitting there with his back to her, holding his rod and gazing at the horizon.

Maybe that would make a good picture, Connie thought suddenly, noticing how the marsh spread around him like a shining backdrop. She raised her camera and took the picture slowly and carefully, as she had seen Stella do, then took another of the Canada geese. One of them was dabbling in the water for food, with his head submerged and his white rump tipped up.

Not wanting to go past the fisherman and disturb him, she turned back the way she had come and finally reached the long slope below the bluff. Halfway up to the top, she paused to look down at the marsh. Off in the distance she could see something on the water that resembled a low, white island. She'd have to find out what that was. She should have asked Stella where the swans were, too.

As Connie turned to climb the rest of the way up, she glimpsed a face peering down at her from the clump of pine trees.

It was the face of a young, shaggy-haired boy. She scrambled quickly to the top of the bluff, but when she got there, he was gone. On the ground she could see the imprint of his sneakers, though, as well as some other tracks that looked like a baby's hand and foot prints.

Slowly she walked back to the house, holding her feathers with care and wondering who the boy was. How could he have disappeared so fast, as if he were some wild creature? And what about the other tracks?

At supper that evening, Dan announced that he was going to set up his telescope so that he could get started on his astronomy project. "Hope I can see something," he muttered in a worried tone.

"Didn't you say that the stars would be brighter here? There ought to be lots to see," Connie said.

"Yes, but what I'm looking for is still pretty low on the horizon at this time of year."

"Oh, some kind of moon, isn't it?"

"Jupiter's moons—the four that Galileo discovered," he explained in his big-brother manner. "Actually Jupiter has many moons, but with a small telescope like mine, you can barely see the others." He shook his head dolefully. "Hope I can find them. Wish I could get up on the roof somehow."

"Now, Dan," Mother began anxiously.

He gave her a reassuring glance. "No, don't worry."

Connie waited in silence, hoping Dan would invite her to come along, but he didn't. Sadly, she remembered the time she'd dropped his star charts and almost lost one of them.

After it got dark, she watched Dan carry his telescope outside and set it up behind the house. He fiddled with it for a while and then folded it up and went off in the direction of the marsh. Connie stayed in the living room, trying to read and wondering how he was doing.

It seemed like a long while, but finally he returned, frowning darkly. "Can't even find Jupiter," he fumed. "And tomorrow will probably be cloudy." He stamped up the stairs to his room.

Connie watched him go, remembering what Stella had said about her older brother being her best friend. She and Dan used to be like that. But all of a sudden now, he seemed to be so much older and smarter than she was.

We used to do everything together, she thought wistfully. Will we ever be good friends again?

That evening before she went to bed, Connie stepped out onto the balcony, wondering if she might see or hear anything tonight, and not at all sure that she wanted to. But the darkened woods and sea lay peaceful under the starry sky. A full moon was beginning to rise, and it hung just above the treetops. Its round white face seemed more brilliant than she could ever remember seeing it anywhere else, and when she went back into her room, she left the draperies open so she could lie in bed and watch it.

Much later, deep in the night, she awoke. As she slid out of a dream, she sensed something—somewhere— that was disturbing. She half-opened her eyes, and in the stillness she heard a distant sound.

There it was again: a grating whisper of metal against metal, then silence. She blinked drowsily at the moonlight pouring into her room and wondered about the noise.

Out on the balcony, a shadow moved slowly past her windows. It was the figure of a man, outlined black and silver in the moonlight. He seemed to have come from the other end of the house.

Alarmed, she half-rose on one elbow, and then she heard his footsteps pause at her balcony door. She sank back, frozen under the blankets.

A small scraping noise came from very close by. He must be turning her doorknob—had she forgotten to lock it?

The door swung open. She saw the odd, squashed-flat features of his face as he stepped into her room, and a scream died in her throat. She closed her eyes.

Would he see her lying here in the shadowed corner? She could hear his ragged breathing, loud in the quiet room, and knew that he was staring at her. She made herself breathe slowly and softly in spite of the wild pounding of her heart.

At last he moved: footsteps padded lightly on the bare floor, and the harsh breathing faded away from her. Something creaked. She heard a series of smooth, sliding sounds, as if a window were being raised, then silence. Puzzled, she waited through another long minute before she opened her eyes. Where was he?

Turning her head slowly on the pillow, she searched the dark corners of her room. He'd gone—that much was certain. The green rocking chair against one wall had been moved aside, but that was all. He must have slipped back out to the balcony without her knowing it. Cautiously she sat up in bed.

From the room next to hers came a muffled thump, followed by a crash, a woman's voice, and a jumble of noises. A door slammed and she heard running feet out on the balcony.

Connie jumped from her bed. She reached her balcony door just as a man rushed past and disappeared from sight.

Chapter Five
Aunt Laura's Secret

By the time Connie got there, Stella was standing at the balcony rail, looking down at the ground.

"I almost had him," she muttered to Connie. "But I didn't know if he had a gun. He must have climbed up this thing." She pulled at the thick, leafless strands of a vine that curled up the side of the house. "It's wisteria—strong as a rope."

"What was that man doing?" Connie whispered, shivering in the cold night air.

"Trying to steal something from your uncle's study, I'm sure," answered Stella. "Not a very smart burglar, if you ask me, making all that noise. It's a good thing Laura gave me a key."

She tightened the belt of the silky green robe that she wore, and she smiled at Connie. "Come on in—we're freezing out here."

Once inside Connie's room, Stella closed the balcony door and locked it.

"I saw him," Connie said hoarsely. Just remembering made her feel shaky, and the words choked in her throat. "I heard him—it was terrible—he—"

"I know. He scared me too. Ugh! That stocking mask!" exclaimed Stella. "Now listen, I don't want to wake up this whole house. You get on back to bed, and I'll take care of that vase he knocked over."

She gave Connie a gentle push toward her bed and Connie was glad to go. Stella smoothed the blanket over her, adding softly, "Better not say anything about this unless someone asks. I don't know what's going on here, but Laura has plenty of things on her mind as it is. When I get a chance, I'll tell your mother what happened."

"Okay," agreed Connie. Mother wouldn't worry so much if Stella was the one who told her about it. Stella gave her an approving pat and left without making a sound.

Connie buried her face in the comforting softness of her pillow. It was a good thing that Stella had a room right next to the study. Her mind felt hazy, as if she had just awakened from a nightmare. She wanted to figure out how much of it had really happened, but confusing black and silver images chased themselves round and round through her mind until at last she gave up trying to think about anything. It was a long time before she fell asleep.

The next morning when Connie took breakfast in to Aunt Laura, she had a feeling that the cheery little woman knew something about the break-in, although she didn't look at all disturbed.

"Why don't you join me again for some cocoa?" Aunt Laura's smile was hard to resist, and Connie quickly got another cup.

It wasn't until after they'd each had two cups of cocoa and Connie had helped Aunt Laura finish her cinnamon toast that the question came. "Tell me what happened up there last night," she said calmly.

"I guess somebody wanted to get into that room next to mine, but Stella chased him away," Connie said. She still wasn't sure if the rest was a dream or not.

When Dan had asked, she'd started to explain about the man coming into her bedroom. But she'd stopped when she saw the look on his face—he thought she'd made it up. And it didn't really make any sense, even to her.

"I should have known that man would come back." Aunt Laura twirled her spoon thoughtfully, and Connie couldn't help thinking that if this were her mother, she'd be terribly upset. What made Aunt Laura so different? This wasn't the gloomy woman that Dan had described.

"Can I do anything for you?" Connie asked sympathetically.

"Yes, you can." Aunt Laura reached for the Bible on her bedside table. "My eyes are getting worse all the time. Would you like to read something to me? Let's see; what shall we have?"

She half-closed her eyes to think about it, and she had an expression on her face that reminded Connie of trying to choose between desserts at a church supper. "How about Psalm 27?"

"Sure." Connie began to read with enthusiasm, glad that she had always been a good reader in school. *The Lord is my light and my salvation; whom shall I fear? the Lord is the strength of my life; of whom shall I be afraid?*"

"That's a good one for me," exclaimed Aunt Laura. "Go on."

Connie read to the end of the psalm, and when she finished, Aunt Laura's face was glowing. "I think I'm going to memorize some of those verses," she said. "They're just what I need right now."

She paused, her bright eyes studying Connie. After a minute, she seemed to have made up her mind about something. "Do you like secrets?" she asked.

Surprised, Connie nodded.

"Well, I have a prayer secret. I'll share it with you if you'd like, and maybe we can pray about it together."

"Oh, yes," Connie said.

"It's about this house."

Connie felt a little disappointed. That didn't sound like anything very exciting to pray about.

But Aunt Laura's gaze was resting fondly on the tall windows that looked out toward the trees. "I have a dream or a hope—or whatever you want to call it. I'd like this house to belong to a mission board that I know, so they can use it as a place for missionaries to rest when they come home on furlough."

She glanced at Connie, her eyes sparkling now. "Think how they'd enjoy the woods and the marsh— how refreshed they could be!"

Connie thought about it. "But where would you live?"

"I'm sure they'd let me stay here as long as I wanted to. There's plenty of room." A shadow crossed Aunt Laura's face. "The problem is that I want to make it a gift, free and clear, but because of something that happened last winter, I still owe some money on the house."

Connie waited, hoping she'd explain.

Aunt Laura took a sip of cocoa and went on. "Last January we had a tremendous snowstorm, and the snow was so heavy that some of our trees fell over. Two of those big, old pine trees smashed into the end of the house where your bedroom is. They did considerable damage, and it cost a lot to have it repaired."

"That's the money you still owe?" asked Connie.

"Yes, that's it." Aunt Laura pulled herself upright on her pillows. "But there's something else that might be part of this. I've had an offer from a man who wants to buy this property—some developer from Atlantic City. I think he's connected with the casinos and he'd pay quite a bit for it. But I don't want to sell it to him." She frowned. "I almost wonder if these strange happenings are supposed to scare me into changing my mind."

She glanced at Connie, and the frown disappeared. "Anyway, that's it. I'm praying that the Lord will somehow enable me to give this house to the mission. Would you like to join me?"

Connie nodded. "Sure, I'll help you pray."

Aunt Laura took Connie's hand into her soft, plump fingers. "Remember—it's our secret. You can't say anything to anybody about it, except the Lord. Okay? We're going to see what He'll do." She gave Connie's hand a friendly squeeze before releasing it. "Let's talk to Him now."

Aunt Laura prayed aloud, and Connie decided that it was the liveliest prayer she had ever heard. She'd been a Christian for two years now, but she'd never thought of prayer as being a conversation with God. Aunt Laura sounded as though she were talking to a dear friend, someone who was right there with them in the room.

Just as she finished, Mother knocked on the half-opened door.

"Don't forget," Aunt Laura whispered to Connie.

"I won't," Connie whispered back.

"What are you two whispering about?" asked Mother, sounding preoccupied.

"Our secret," Aunt Laura said, and Connie grinned.

But Mother didn't seem to be listening. She looked worried, Connie thought. Had Stella talked to her yet about last night? Maybe she hadn't had a chance.

Mother came closer. "Laura, did you hear that commotion in the middle of the night? What was it?"

"Apparently someone tried to break into my husband's study," Aunt Laura said quietly. "Stella frightened him away."

"Oh, that's terrible. Are we going to call the police?"

Aunt Laura sounded as if she were discussing the weather. "Probably not. But we could mention it to Mr. Stafford if you like. He might be able to check around outside. Perhaps that vine should be cut down."

"I'll phone him right away." Connie's mother bustled out of the room, adding over her shoulder, "Connie, I could use some help in the kitchen."

Connie hurried through the breakfast dishes and ran upstairs. Before anyone came to investigate, she wanted to take a look at that balcony by daylight.

This morning, with sunlight slanting across it, the long balcony looked cheerful and ordinary. Connie leaned out over the railing to tug at the vine. Some of its branches were as thick as her arm, and they twisted up the supporting posts to cover the whole end of the balcony. There were only a few broken strands to show where the thief had climbed up and down.

As she straightened up, she noticed a torn piece of something blue, caught on a rusty nail. Eagerly she pulled it off and studied it. Not much of a clue, but—

"What've you got there?" Dan asked from behind her.

"Just this." She held up the scrap of blue nylon fabric. Dan dismissed it with a glance. "Did you really see the guy?" he asked. "What did he look like?"

"Well, Stella said he had on a stocking mask, so no one could tell anything about his face," she began.

"I mean, was he tall or short? Fat or thin?"

"I'm not sure," she answered lamely. "It was all so rushed and dark. He wasn't real big. Sort of medium everything, I guess."

"Medium everything?" Dan gave her a look that made her feel like a six-year-old. He bent over the balcony railing as Connie had done. "Hey, that guy might have left some tracks down there," he said. "Let's go see."

They clattered down the stairs, only to find Mr. Stafford standing in the front hall. He was talking excitedly to Mother about the burglary attempt. He interrupted himself to smile at them. "Going to look for clues, kiddies? I've already checked out there. Nothing to be seen, I'm afraid, nothing at all."

Dan murmured something polite, edging past the two grown-ups, and Connie followed. They slipped around the house to the corner of the porch.

Dan knelt to look at the ground near the base of the vine and exclaimed in disappointment. "Huh! I'll say this much for him—if there were any tracks, he's certainly messed them up."

Connie studied the boot prints that cut deeply into the soft earth of the flower bed, and she had to agree with Dan. "I guess he'd have noticed anything that was here," she said hopefully. "He sure does have big feet."

She lowered her voice as she caught sight of her mother and Mr. Stafford coming toward them.

Mr. Stafford was nodding vigorously, and his spiky white hair seemed to bristle with energy. "Sure, I can do it, if that's what Laura wants. I'll be back later on in the afternoon. If she still thinks the vine should be cut down, I'll take care of it. I certainly will." He raised his hand in a half-salute and sauntered down the path to the salt marsh.

It wasn't until after lunch that Connie remembered to tell Aunt Laura about yesterday's phone call from the museum.

For a minute Aunt Laura looked confused; then she shrugged her shoulders. "My husband, Philip, was a great shell collector. We had missionary friends who sent us shells from all over the world. It's possible that Philip talked to some museum about his cowrie shells, but I don't know about that. He was full of surprises."

She smiled at Connie. "You can look at the shells anytime, if you like that sort of thing. They're in a closet in his study. He has a lot of books there too, if you need some information for your school project."

Connie's interest quickened at the thought of a room full of books. "It's locked, isn't it?" she asked, hoping Aunt Laura would give her a key like the one Stella had.

Aunt Laura's blue eyes twinkled. "You mean you haven't discovered his secret door?"

"No, what do you mean?"

"Philip loved puzzles and secret things. The room you're sleeping in used to be our bedroom. He figured out a way to hide a connecting door in the wall between our bedroom and his study." Aunt Laura's dimples deepened. "You'll have to see if you can find it."

"Okay," Connie agreed happily. She had always liked puzzles, too. If she could find that door, it would be even better than having a key.

"Maybe you could do something for me while you're in his study," added Aunt Laura. "There is one of his shells that I can't seem to find: it's called a golden cowrie. You might keep an eye open for it." Her voice trailed off. "I haven't gone through his desk yet . . . all those papers. . . ."

Connie wanted to ask what a golden cowrie looked like, but Aunt Laura's face was pale and drawn, as if talking so much had worn her out. "I'll try to find it," she promised, and left Aunt Laura to rest.

As she passed the kitchen, her mother called, "Connie, will you come and stir this for me?"

"What is it?" Connie joined her mother at the stove and swirled a spoon through the thin, milky-colored mixture in the pot.

"It's a custard filling. Don't stop stirring and don't let it burn."

Connie licked off a drop that had spattered onto her hand. "Mm-mm, good. What's it for?"

"I'm making chocolate eclairs. Laura said Mr. Stafford likes to eat (I could tell that, Connie thought), and he might feel like a snack after he's finished cutting down that vine for us."

"Oh, those are so good—I hope you're making a lot of them," Connie said.

When the custard was done, she helped her mother for a while longer, just in case some of the eclair shells turned out bad and had to be eaten right away. But all of them came plump and golden from the oven, quite worthy of the custard filling.

After Connie had licked every trace of chocolate icing from the bowl and had washed the dishes, her mother asked, "What are you going to do with yourself this afternoon?"

Connie had planned to go upstairs and look for the secret door into the study, but she didn't want to tell anybody about it yet. Quickly she changed her mind. "I guess I'll go hunt up some feathers for my collection," she told her mother. "Maybe I'll find some in Deer Meadow by those birdhouses."

She took an apple for nibbling on later and picked up her camera. The secret door would have to wait.

When she stepped into the pine woods beside the house, she couldn't help thinking about the wolf-dog she had seen there. At least she thought she had seen it. What about the dead bird and those dog tracks in the mud, though? There certainly must be some kind of wild animal roaming around. It was surprisingly dark under the pine trees, and the gloom was filled with mysterious rustlings and twitterings that made her hurry along the path.

At the edge of Deer Meadow, she climbed across the fallen wire fence and stopped to take a picture. As she finished, she heard rapid footsteps behind her. She turned. A young boy with mud-caked boots was running down the path from the pine woods.

"Watch out," he panted as he neared her. "There's a wild dog—coming." He stumbled across the old fence.

Connie reached out to steady him. "Where is it?"

"Hurry!" The boy glanced fearfully over his shoulder, and Connie looked too. A huge, shaggy dog was trotting purposefully through the pine trees toward them.

Chapter Six
Escape

Suddenly Connie remembered the Lookout Tree. "C'mon, there's a tree over here." She grabbed for the boy's hand and ran at full speed across the meadow, dragging him with her. It took only seconds to reach the tree and climb the ladder.

"There he comes!" exclaimed the boy.

Connie looked back. Now the animal was loping across the meadow, and she could see that it looked more like a big brown dog than a wolf.

It soon caught up with them and jumped up against the tree, stretching its muddy paws high on the trunk. When Connie leaned over the edge of the platform for a better look, it stared up at her, growling deep in its throat, and she hoped fervently that dogs couldn't climb ladders. It was so close that she could see the torn edge of one ear.

"He chased after me," the boy said unsteadily. "And I tried wading across a mud flat, but I couldn't lose him."

He pulled the remains of a bologna sandwich from his jacket pocket and looked at it regretfully. "I didn't even get to finish my sandwich." He took a huge bite of it, not seeming to care that the bread was crumpled and greasy. The strong odor of garlic made Connie's nose twitch.

"I can smell that thing over here," she exclaimed from the other side of the platform. "No wonder the dog went after you."

The boy shrugged, and he wiped one hand across the grimy front of his jacket.

"Why don't we throw it down to him? Then maybe he'll go away," she persisted.

"But I'm hungry," he mumbled, chewing faster.

Connie glanced down at the dog, and it gazed back at her with burning eyes. "Well, maybe he's starving. How'd you like it if we have to sit here all night? You'd better let me give it to him."

The boy stuffed the rest of the sandwich into his mouth and reached slowly into his pocket. "Here's my last one," he said grudgingly, handing her a sodden mass of bread and meat.

Connie threw it hard, as far away from the tree as she could.

The dog bounded over to the food, gulped it down, and then circled through the grass, looking for more.

"Go home!" Connie yelled. It looked up at her, as if it had heard those words before, but it took a couple of steps closer to the tree.

Connie reached above her head and broke off a dead branch. She waved it threateningly and shouted again. "Bad dog! Go home! Go home!"

The dog did not retreat, but it began snuffling through the grass again until it seemed to find something interesting. Then it trotted off slowly, its nose to the ground.

The boy stood silent, watching the dog go, and Connie had a chance to look at him more closely. Although he was small and scrawny, she guessed that he must be almost her age. Under the shaggy mop of hair, his eyes had the alert, wary expression that she had once seen on a captured fox.

He shook his head, muttering, "I've heard of them, but I never thought I'd see one."

"One what?"

"One of them wild dogs. I'll bet that's what he is, too. They run in packs in the Pine Barrens, and everybody's afraid of them."

"But this isn't the Pine Barrens," she pointed out.

"Close enough. See that?" He waved a hand toward the wide sweep of trees that stretched behind them. "Just a couple of miles that way—those woods join onto the Pine Barrens."

He turned and regarded her gravely. "This tree was a good idea. I'd forgotten about it. I'm Ricky. What's your name? How come you're here?"

"I'm Connie. We came to visit the lady in that house over there. Laura Hendrick." As she spoke, Connie noticed how thin the boy's face was, and she took out the apple she'd brought along. "Here, since I gave away your food, would you like this?"

"Sure." He took it quickly, almost snatching it from her hand, and shoved it into the same greasy pocket that had held his sandwiches.

As he turned toward the edge of the platform, Connie said, "Hey, you'd better get your mother to wash that coat so our friend doesn't come sniffing after you any more." She meant it for a joke, but he didn't smile.

"My mother's gone," he said soberly, and began climbing down the ladder.

Connie watched him until he was out of sight, and she wondered about his mother. After taking a picture of the view from the platform, she decided it was time to leave. The chocolate eclairs would be ready by now, and she wanted to tell her mother about Ricky. Too bad she hadn't taken a picture of that dog.

By the time she reached the house, however, Mr. Stafford was already sitting in Aunt Laura's bedroom with a cup of coffee. He must have finished cutting down the vine.

Mother was busy working on sandwiches in the kitchen, and she glanced up, looking relieved. "You got here just in time. Please take these in and pass them around."

Connie noticed that Dan had made an appearance too. He was sitting near Mr. Stafford with an expectant, hungry look on his face.

After she had served Aunt Laura, Connie turned to Mr. Stafford. "Would you like to try one of these, sir?" She offered him the plate of sandwiches with what she hoped was a gracious smile.

Dan reached over and helped himself. "Thank you, Princess Sis," he said with a teasing grin.

She jerked the plate away from him, feeling her cheeks tingle with embarrassment. He always called her that when she was doing her best to act grown-up. After Mr. Stafford had taken a handful of the tiny sandwiches, she sat down near Aunt Laura and shot a reproving glance at Dan.

But he seemed to be listening to Mr. Stafford tell about all the years he had lived in New Jersey and how he was going to move to Arizona.

"Beautiful, beautiful Arizona," Mr. Stafford repeated. "I'm really looking forward to it." He talked on and on. Connie nibbled impatiently on a sandwich. All this time she could have been upstairs, looking for the secret door. And the afternoon was almost gone.

Mother must have been thinking the same thing, for she jumped up and brought in the tray of eclairs. "Wouldn't you like one of these before you go?" she asked.

Mr. Stafford's eyes gleamed. "Oh, what a wonderful sight. You certainly are a treasure, Mrs. Lawrence. My mother used to make these—" He picked up an eclair and bit into it so hard that the custard filling spurted onto his chin. "Just delicious—" He wiped it off with the back of his hand and kept talking while Connie and Dan exchanged amused glances.

Finally, after eating a second eclair and drinking another cup of coffee, he hauled himself to his feet. "Thank you, ladies," he said in his flowery way. "Thank you indeed."

On his way to the front door, he remarked, "Well, I hope we have some peace and quiet around here this evening. Did you hear those teen-agers with their motorcycles last night?"

"No," Mother said politely, opening the door for him. "Were they over by your house?"

"Yes, I'm closer to the highway. That must be why I heard them." He stopped. "Well now, will you listen to that?"

On the breeze from the marsh came the rising clamor of several engines in chorus. "Of all things! They must be over at the bird refuge." Mr. Stafford zipped up his jacket and stepped briskly through the doorway. "I'm going to see about this," he exclaimed.

"Hey, Connie." Dan was behind her. "Let's find out what's happening."

They grabbed their jackets and followed Mr. Stafford's rolling stride down the path that Connie had taken the day before. Before long they reached the sandy bluff that overlooked the marsh.

Mr. Stafford was staring angrily into the pale winter dusk. Above the snarl of motorcycles came the sound of frenzied bird cries. In the distance, Connie could see great clouds of birds rising and settling and rising again.

"They're riding around on the dikes with those motorcycles, that's what they're doing," Mr. Stafford muttered. "They'll frighten the birds half to death." He swung around to stare disapprovingly at Connie and Dan. "Teen-agers! Ought to be locked up, the whole bunch of them. I wouldn't be surprised if one of them was your burglar. I'm going to call the police." He stumped off down the path and disappeared into the twilight.

"Race you back to the house," offered Dan.

"Not this time," Connie said. "I'll just stay here for a couple of minutes." She had glimpsed Stella's slim figure walking up from the marsh and hoped for a chance to talk with her. As soon as Dan left, Connie scrambled down the bluff.

Stella's bright eyes were snapping, and Connie was thankful not to be the object of her anger. "Those kids are going to get into real trouble," Stella exclaimed.

She shook her head, making the gold hoops in her ears dance. "They think they're so smart, racing around out there so they can watch the birds fly."

"Mr. Stafford said they were on the dikes. What's he mean?"

"The dikes are long banks of earth and stones," Stella explained. "In the refuge they use dikes to keep the freshwater ponds separate from the salt marsh. That way a lot of different birds will come here. The dikes are wide enough for people to drive on, and they come out in their cars to watch the birds."

As she spoke, Stella looked back at the marsh, where birds were still wheeling in disordered circles. "Most people are careful not to disturb them."

She gave Connie a quick glance. "When was Mr. Stafford talking to you?"

"He came over to cut down that vine this afternoon and then stayed to visit with Aunt Laura," Connie told her. "You know, he's funny, the way he acts—almost as if he were in a play or something."

"Hmm," was all Stella said as they turned to walk up to the house, but Connie had the feeling that she didn't particularly admire Mr. Stafford. He *was* a little odd, Connie thought, but at least he cared about the birds.

"Were you taking some more pictures?" she asked, glancing at Stella's camera.

"Yes, from the photo blind. I spend a lot of time there. Next time you're out in the marsh, bring your camera over, and maybe you can get some close-ups."

"The photo blind?"

"Yes, it's a place where you can watch the birds and take pictures without their seeing you," Stella explained.

"I especially like the one in the refuge—it's so hidden away you'd hardly know it's there. Good place for a smuggler's hideout."

Connie had to grin at that. Stella must like reading mysteries as much as she did.

Stella tore a page from her notebook. "Here, I'll show you where it is." She sketched a map as she spoke. "See, the dikes go around like this, and there's a gravel road here—then a path comes off this way. Just follow the path through the woods, all the way out to the water. You'll see the photo blind."

She handed the page to Connie with a friendly smile. "I'm going into town tomorrow to get some film developed. Do you have any that you'd like me to take in for you?"

"Yes, I sure do. I just finished my second roll today," Connie said. By now they had reached the porch, and she added, "It must be nearly supper time. I'll get them for you right away."

Up in her room, she sorted through the pile of books and papers that had accumulated on her bedside table. That first roll of film had been here just the other day. At least she knew for sure where the other one was. Carefully she removed it from her camera and then took another look around the room for the missing film. Well, she'd get this one developed for now.

As she started to leave, she glanced curiously at the wall that separated her room from the study. That secret door must be hidden there somewhere.

All through supper she thought about it, and as soon as she'd finished helping with the dishes, she ran upstairs.

Chapter Seven
The Secret Door

First Connie examined the wall. It was covered with large and small rectangles of dark, polished wood that were arranged in a geometric pattern. She studied the longer panels. It seemed most likely that a door would be hidden behind one of them, but they all looked the same. Well, there was only one way to find out.

She started in the middle and ran her fingers over each long panel that she could reach. She felt along the raised wood edges; then she pressed and poked and tugged. Finally a panel slid sideways. Behind it was a narrow space several feet high. Eagerly she felt along the back wall of the opening. Perhaps the next panel would work the same way. It slid open obediently when she pressed the right corner, and she stepped through the wall with a sense of triumph.

She found herself at one end of a small room that seemed to be bare. It was dimly lit by the light from her bedroom, but she quickly found a switch and turned on the overhead light. After some experimenting, she figured out how to make the wall panels slide shut behind her. Now she could explore.

This doesn't look like a study, she thought, gazing around herself at rows and rows of built-in drawers. This was more like an oversize closet. Of course. Hadn't Aunt Laura told her that Philip Hendrick's shell collection was in a closet?

Connie pulled open the nearest drawer. It was filled with neatly arranged shells. They looked interesting, but she could come back to them later. She crossed to the door and opened it.

Light from the closet streamed into another, longer room, revealing a roll-top desk and walls that were lined with books. She smiled to herself. Now here was a real study.

She roamed around the room, its red carpet soft under her feet, and scanned the books on the shelves. There were all kinds—fiction, history, science. She saw several books about shells and a whole shelf of bird books. On a narrow ledge above the desk stood a row of small spiral-bound notebooks. When she peeked into one of them, she saw that it was some kind of journal or diary.

She stopped beside the desk, remembering that Aunt Laura had asked her to try to find that certain shell called a golden cowrie. Of course it might be mixed in with all those other shells, but if it was special, someone might have put it in here.

Hesitantly she rolled back the top of the desk. It had two rows of pigeonholes, places where a shell could be hidden. A handful of papers had been thrust into the first compartment, and as she pulled them out, the return address on the top envelope caught her eye: TRANS WORLD MARITIME MUSEUM. Wasn't that the name of the place that the man on the phone had mentioned? And he had talked about a cowrie shell.

The envelope, addressed to Philip Hendrick, had already been opened. After staring at the letter for another minute, she decided to read it in case it said something that would help her to find the shell.

The letter did mention the golden cowrie. It even referred to an offer the museum had made to purchase it. They wanted to know what his final decision was because they were anxious to include the shell in their next exhibit. It was signed *Jason Ross.*

Thoughtfully Connie folded up the letter, wondering why Philip Hendrick hadn't answered it. She unfolded it again to check the date: February 12. That was the month before he died. Maybe he hated writing letters as much as she did. She glanced at the notebooks lined up above the desk. Those diaries might tell what had happened. Maybe Aunt Laura would let her read them.

She wandered back to the row of books about shells. She really ought to find out what a golden cowrie looked like. It must be something special if a museum wanted to buy it. She found a book titled *Sea Treasures* that had several paragraphs about the different kinds of cowrie shells. Apparently the golden cowrie could be found near islands in the Pacific Ocean, usually in deep water. The book described it as "beautiful and rare."

She stopped reading in order to study the photographs on the facing page. The golden cowrie was a medium-sized shell with a rounded back; its color was a deep golden orange. Even in the picture it glowed like a jewel. If Philip Hendrick had one of those, no wonder the museum wanted to buy it.

"Connie?" She could hear Dan's voice. It sounded as if he were standing at her bedroom door. Still holding the shell book, she quickly rolled the desk top closed and went to open the door of the study. "I'm in here," she said.

Dan walked down to join her, curiosity written all over his face. "How come? What're you doing?"

"Aunt Laura said I could look at the books."

Dan followed her back into the room and whistled in surprise. "That's right. I'd forgotten he had all these books." He gazed hungrily at the crowded shelves. "Do you think she'd care if I read some of them?"

"I doubt it. Look in here—he's got a whole closet full of shells." Connie pulled open a drawer of shells to show Dan. Happily, she recognized their shiny humped backs. "See, these are cowries," she told him, proud of her new knowledge. "I wonder what kind," she murmured, flipping back to the picture in her book.

Dan nodded absent-mindedly. "Yes, that's sure a big collection." He stepped back into the study to examine the books on the shelves. "He's got some of everything! The science stuff is outdated, but there's a bunch of other good ones. Maybe I'll take a couple back to my room."

Dan made his choices quickly. Connie decided to keep the shell book and come back later for another book. When Dan left, she followed him out into the hall instead of using the secret door. She wouldn't tell him about it—not right now, anyway.

Once back in her room, she regarded the paneled wall with satisfaction. It was fun having her own secret entrance to that room full of books. She started to straighten the rocking chair that she'd pushed aside when she was searching for the door, and then she stopped short.

Last night, after that man had been in here, this same chair had been left out of place. Her mind began to race. No wonder she hadn't heard him go back out to the balcony. Connie dropped onto her bed to think it through.

First, he must have tried to unlock the balcony door to the study: that was the faraway noise she had heard. Then he'd given up, come into her room, and used the secret door.

She sat up with a jerk. How had he found out about that door, anyway? He'd have to be somebody who knew the house very well. It was a creepy thought. She jumped up to make sure that her door to the balcony was locked and then slowly began getting ready for bed.

Later, after Mother had left and she was settled down for the night, Connie decided to begin praying about Aunt Laura's request. When she had finished, an idea crept into her mind. That golden cowrie must be worth a lot of money. If she could find it, then the museum would buy it, and Aunt Laura could pay off the debt on her house. It would be the perfect way for the Lord to answer her prayer.

It was a wonderful idea. She'd start by searching through the whole study. And first thing tomorrow, she'd find out from Aunt Laura if she could read those diaries.

She fell asleep thinking about another reason that she wanted to find the shell. Dan would be pretty impressed, wouldn't he? Yes. And then he might not think of her as such a little kid anymore.

The next morning while they sipped cocoa together, Connie asked Aunt Laura about the diaries.

Aunt Laura waved a plump hand to dismiss the question. "Read anything you like in that room, my dear. I'm afraid those journals won't be very interesting, though. Philip used them to keep track of his bird sightings." She wrinkled up her nose in a comical grimace. "Rather dull stuff if you ask me. And his writing is so small and squiggly—I can hardly read it anymore."

She sighed, as if in regret, and Connie wished that she had already found the shell so she could hand it to Aunt Laura right then. That would cheer her up. There was something else to ask, though, something she had been wondering about. What if she couldn't find the shell and there was no other way to get money for the house?

"Aunt Laura," she began, "you know how we're praying about this house? What if it isn't God's will for you to give the house to the mission? What if He doesn't send the money?"

Aunt Laura nodded. "That's a good question. We keep saying 'God answers prayer,' but sometimes we forget that He might tell us *no* or *wait* instead of *yes.*"

She put her cup on the bedside table and opened her Bible to a blue bookmark in the Psalms. "Remember when you read Psalm 27 for me? I'm trying to memorize it. I haven't learned the last part yet, and it's really good: *"Wait on the Lord: be of good courage, and he shall strengthen thine heart: wait, I say, on the Lord."*

Aunt Laura smiled then, a remembering sort of smile. "I used to worry all the time, and it made me complain a lot. In fact, my husband said I was turning into a grouchy old woman. Then I found out that God doesn't mean for Christians to just muddle through their lives as best they can. And the more I read the Bible, the more I realize that He has something special for each of us."

Slowly she closed her Bible and put it back on the bedside table. "Since then, I've been talking to the Lord about the things that bother me, and as long as I stay close to Him, He shows me what to do. Sometimes His answers have been different from what I wanted, but I'm learning not to fuss about that."

Aunt Laura's gaze was steady and reassuring. "All I know for sure about the house problem is that I can trust Him to do what's best. I'd like to think that it would be His will for the mission to have this house, but I guess we'll know for certain when He answers."

Connie wasn't sure she understood everything Aunt Laura had told her, but she liked the calm, confident way she'd said, "when He answers." Watching her aunt's serene face, Connie had the sudden thought that this confidence must be the reason Aunt Laura had changed from the way Dan remembered her.

After they had prayed together, Connie gathered up the breakfast things, her mind still on the missing shell. Selling the golden cowrie really would be a perfect way to get the money Aunt Laura needed. Since it was raining outside, this morning would be a good time to look for it. But when she carried the breakfast tray back to the kitchen, she found that her mother was energetically paging through a cookbook.

She must be getting ready for another one of her baking days, Connie thought. Mother usually took off on a baking spree when her painting wasn't going well; it helped her mind get unstuck, she said. Whatever the cause, Connie could always tell that it was baking day by the mess in the kitchen and the wonderful aromas that drifted through the house.

Mother usually asked Connie to help her, too, and today was no different. "What are we making?" Connie asked, resigning herself to a morning in the kitchen.

"Oh, cinnamon buns and chocolate cookies, to start with," her mother said vaguely. "Then maybe a pie. Would you see if you can find some cookie sheets for me?"

Although Connie always liked to help with Mother's baking projects, everything seemed to take longer than usual this morning. When the last bowl was washed, she dried her hands and edged toward the kitchen door. She'd been thinking about that shell all morning. Maybe now she'd get a chance to look for it.

She entered the study through the secret door and stopped to gaze thoughtfully at the drawers of shells all around her. Perhaps she'd better make sure that the golden cowrie wasn't in here somewhere. One by one she opened the drawers and began searching through them.

Philip Hendrick seemed to have collected shells of every size and color, and he had labeled each kind. There were limpets, which looked like little hats, and turretillas, like tiny pointed towers, and a whole drawer of lovely pearl-lined saucers, called abalones. But some of the shells were strange rather than beautiful, Connie thought, like the scorpion conch, which had odd, prickly-looking legs sticking out from its lower edge.

By the time she reached the fifth drawer, she had decided that the cowrie shells were her favorites. They came with all kinds of beautiful markings, but each one had a rounded, glossy back and, on the bottom side, an interesting slit with toothed ridges that curled inward. She cradled a tiger cowrie in one hand, admiring its pattern of rich brown dots. It felt cool and smooth, and she held it for a minute longer, wondering if this was how the golden cowrie would feel when she found it.

Suddenly impatient with herself, she put the tiger cowrie back into its tissue-lined drawer. Standing here dreaming wasn't going to find that shell. Maybe she'd see if the diaries had anything interesting to say. She could look through the rest of the drawers another time.

She turned toward the study, where the diaries stood waiting for her, their spiral-bound backs stiffly upright.

Chapter Eight
Ricky and Coon

As she took the diaries down a few at a time, Connie discovered that each one was neatly labeled with a beginning and ending date. The first volume was green, the second yellow, the third green, and so on, with green and yellow covers alternating through the whole set of a dozen or more.

She opened one at random. It was filled with notes that were just what Aunt Laura had described.

3/30 Saw 2 Sh-T. Sparrows and 1 H. Merganser in marsh; Barred Owl, Goshawk, many finches, crows, bluej. in woods. At Gull Pond, an Iceland Gull, not sure. Rainy all day.

The small, precise handwriting went on, page after page, interrupted only by a new date or a comment on the weather.

Perhaps a more recent diary would say something else. She picked up the next-to-last volume, a yellow one, and browsed through it. Tucked between the bird notations for September was a sentence with a name in it that caught her eye.

Had a talk with Jason Ross about gc—museum wants it—don't know what to do.

That 'gc' had to refer to the golden cowrie, Connie thought. Her interest quickened, and she skipped impatiently over five more pages of bird notes, hunting for another interesting sentence. Finally she found one on the last page of the diary, dated September 30.

Tatum snooping in shell room; haven't decided about gc; feel like hiding it.

The rest of the page was filled with bird sightings. Connie reached for the next diary, then stopped. The next one should have a green cover, and the only one left was yellow.

The dates in the yellow volume were wrong, too, for it began with January 12 of the next year. It didn't have as many entries as the others. Besides the bird sightings, which included an excited notation about seeing the rare cinnamon teal, there was a curt record of the damage done to the house by the fallen trees. Several weeks later came a sentence that announced Philip Hendrick's decision to sell his sailboat to pay the repair bills. It was dated March 10 and must have been written just before he died, for it was the last entry.

Connie riffled through the blank pages that remained and then put the diary back, feeling sorry for Aunt Laura all over again. She stared at the row of diaries. Where was the green volume that came before this one? Maybe it had been mislaid somehow, on one of the other shelves.

She was still looking for it when she heard her mother's call to lunch. Reluctantly she left the study, hoping that Aunt Laura could tell her where to find the missing diary.

While they ate, Connie studied the sky through the kitchen window, glad to see that pale sunshine was leaking through the clouds. Stella must have noticed it too, for she stopped by the kitchen to say, "Looks like it's clearing up, doesn't it? I spent all morning in town, and I was hoping I could go down to the marsh this afternoon without getting soaked." Her dark eyes met Connie's eager gaze. "Want to come along?"

"Sure," Connie exclaimed.

Later as they stood together on the bluff, Stella pointed to the birds that flew to and fro over the water. "I think there's something wrong with the geese these days. The motorcycles last night didn't help, but even before that the birds seemed nervous about something. They usually don't spook very easily in a refuge."

"Can they tell when they're in a safe place?" asked Connie.

"I think so," Stella answered. "I've studied the way migrating geese behave at bird refuges compared to other places, and they just seem to know."

They started down through the slippery wet grass toward the marsh, and Connie saw the low island of white that she had noticed before. "What's that?" she asked Stella. "It looks like ice or something."

Stella chuckled. "Come on closer and you'll see for yourself. Maybe we won't go to the photo blind just now. The wind isn't as cold as usual today—we'll take a walk along the dike."

On their way to the road that ran along the top of the dikes, they passed a broad hill. A flock of Canada geese were feeding there, gabbling to each other in deep voices as they nipped the winter-brown grass. "Oh, look," exclaimed Connie. "Here come some more."

She watched as five Canada geese circled overhead and honked inquiringly. When the geese on the ground honked back, the newcomers set their wings and glided down, landing nearby. Connie quickly took a picture.

"That flock lives here," Stella explained as they walked along the dike, "but there are lots of other Canada geese that visit the refuge."

Connie stopped to pick up a long, brown tail feather, and she noticed the plumes of marsh grass, rustling in the wind. "These are so pretty." She touched one of the fluffy heads. "There's an arrangement of them in my room. I've been wondering who put it there."

"Well, I thought it would be a right friendly thing to do," Stella said with a smile. "I was hoping Mrs. Atkins hadn't thrown it out while I was at the conference."

"Thanks—I sure like it." Connie smiled up at her, glad that Stella had wanted her to feel welcome. Then she remembered the white island she had come to investigate and glanced ahead. She could see now that it was a huge flock of white birds, floating in one of the larger ponds.

"So that's what it is—there must be hundreds of them!" she exclaimed. "Are they some kind of duck?"

"Snow geese," said Stella. "They come here every fall just about this time—they're on their way south."

The snow geese were busily feeding and preening and calling to each other with hoarse, excited honks. "We won't go any nearer today," cautioned Stella. "No point in making them more nervous than they already are. You'd need a telephoto lens to get any kind of picture. See how far out they are from the shore? Usually they're in much closer."

The nervous geese reminded Connie of the black duck feathers they had found. "You know the tracks we saw the other day?" she asked. "I think I saw the dog that made them. He was awfully big." She couldn't forget about the dog and the boy, Ricky, and now it was a relief to tell someone about it.

They walked back along the dike while she talked, and when Connie finished, Stella nodded. "I think the ranger at the refuge will have to do something about that dog. It must have come down from the Pine Barrens. Dogs like that—they're called feral dogs—often have rabies and can infect other animals. Then, of course, they bother the deer and kill a lot of birds. No wonder the geese are nervous these days."

When they reached the woods above the marsh, Connie caught sight of a ragged figure ahead of them. "Hi, Ricky," she called out. "Wait for me."

She hurried to catch up with the boy, expecting some kind of friendly response. But he stood there solemnly, eyeing her as though he'd never seen her before in his life. Over his shoulder peered the small black-masked face of a young raccoon.

"Hi, Ricky," she repeated, breathless from running up the hill. She reached out to pet the raccoon, but the boy took a step backward, raising a protective hand.

She pretended not to notice his rebuff. "Oh, your raccoon is so cute! I saw some little baby tracks by your footprints the other day—I guess they were his tracks. What's his name?"

"I just call him Coon," the boy muttered.

"Where'd you get him? I didn't see him yesterday."

The boy darted a suspicious glance at Stella, who had joined them. "His mother got shot," he said briefly.

"And yesterday when he saw the dog he took off into the woods."

"We were just talking about that dog!" Connie exclaimed. "Have you seen any more of him?"

"Nope."

"Look, here's a feather I found for my school project. Do you know what kind it is?" Connie asked. She was beginning to feel silly, the way she was rattling on and on, but she wanted to keep him talking.

"Probably Canada goose." The boy turned his back on them and plunged into the trees, the raccoon holding on to his hair with both hands.

Connie stared after him for a minute and then looked at Stella apologetically. "I guess he's just shy. I wonder who he is."

Stella turned onto the trail leading to Aunt Laura's. "He might belong to one of the families that live down the marsh a ways. Most of them are fishermen or clammers."

"He said his mother is gone," Connie told her.

Stella nodded. "No wonder he looks so unkempt. He probably does as he pleases. He might be an interesting person to make friends with, though. I imagine he knows this marsh as well as you know your own backyard."

That evening, right after supper, Dan disappeared outside with his telescope, and Connie went upstairs to work on her journal for school. She spent a long time on a page about the marsh, trying to describe what she'd seen and how it made her feel.

Finally she put down her pen, yawning, and her mind wandered to the roll of film that Stella had taken in to be developed. Even though it wouldn't be ready for a couple of days, she couldn't wait to see how her pictures had turned out. They wouldn't be as good as Stella's, but maybe Stella would give her some tips on how to take really professional ones. Of course Stella had that expensive camera and a telephoto lens.

Connie eyed her little instamatic camera regretfully. It sure would be nice to have a telephoto lens too. She stood up and stretched, deciding to go down to the kitchen to see if there were any brownies left from supper.

On her way to the stairs, she passed the open door of Dan's room and noticed that he had left his camera on the desk. He must be planning to take some pictures too. She stared at his camera curiously, wondering if it had a telephoto lens. Maybe she could talk him into letting her borrow it.

She stepped into his room to take a quick look. Just as she picked up the camera, she heard Dan's feet pounding up the stairs, and she felt a guilty impulse to drop it and run.

But already he stood in the doorway with his telescope. "What're you doing?" he asked.

"I just wanted to see if your camera has a telephoto lens on it," she said, turning it over carefully.

"Yes, it does. You'd better put it down." His face was reddened from the cold wind outside, and Connie could tell by his grim expression that he hadn't found the stars or whatever it was he kept looking for.

Hurriedly she told him, "Stella's camera has a telephoto lens so she can take close-ups of the birds, and I was wondering if I could borrow yours because I want to take some pictures especially for—"

"Forget it," he interrupted, turning away to set down his telescope in a corner.

"Why not?"

He shot her an exasperated glance. "Because you'll break it, that's why. Or it'll fall into a pond or something."

"But I—" she began in protest.

He held up a hand. "Yeah, I know. It's never your fault, but it always happens. And I need to get some homework done now, okay?"

Connie retreated from his room and stalked down the stairs. Someday Dan would wish he'd let her borrow his camera. She sure hoped so, anyway. And meanwhile she was going to win that photo contest, no matter what.

She carried two brownies and a glass of milk up to her room, set them on the bedside table, and took the secret route into the study to find a good book. While she was there, she hunted through several more drawers of shells, but soon gave up in discouragement.

Back in her room, she settled down with a mystery story and her brownies and read until she could hardly keep her eyes open. Reluctantly she began to get ready for bed.

After she'd said good night to Mother and was snug under the blankets at last, she remembered to pray for Aunt Laura's house. In the middle of that, she began to wonder about the missing diary. She hadn't had a chance to ask Aunt Laura about it because her aunt had been away at the doctor's all afternoon and then had been too tired to talk to anyone. While Connie was still thinking about all the things that could happen to a small green book, she fell asleep.

Chapter Nine
In the Photo Blind

During their cocoa time the next morning, Connie told Aunt Laura about the missing diary and asked if she had any idea where it could be.

"Not a clue," she answered with a quick shake of her head. "Philip was always putting things in the most unlikely places. For all I know, he might have had it on the sailboat with him, and it was lost along with everything else."

Connie didn't think that was likely, and she wanted to ask if there might be another place to look for the diary, but a loud knock at the front door interrupted her.

"Sounds like Mr. Stafford," Aunt Laura observed dryly.

A minute later their neighbor stumped into the bedroom with his big fishing boots, and his pink face was more flushed than usual. "Those rascals!" he huffed. "They tried to rob me."

"Sit down," Aunt Laura suggested in her calm manner. "What happened?"

He sank heavily into the armchair by Aunt Laura's bed. "Burglars—last night. I heard them in the middle of the night."

"What did they steal?" asked Connie.

"Nothing." His pale blue eyes gleamed with triumph. "Nothing at all. I chased them off before they could take a thing."

"Oh my, I'm glad you did," soothed Aunt Laura. "Would you like a cup of coffee?"

"Yes, thank you, kind ladies," he answered, sounding more like himself. "Your refreshments are always so delicious." He beamed at Connie's mother when she appeared with the coffee and a plate of cinnamon buns. "Those look wonderful, just wonderful."

He demolished half a bun in one bite and settled back in the chair as if he meant to stay all morning. "You know, Laura, I was working on my shell collection the other day, and it reminded me of dear Philip. He had quite an assortment of cowries, didn't he?"

"Could be," Aunt Laura said vaguely. "Are you going to call the police about this burglary attempt?"

He shook his head and reached for another cinnamon bun. "Wouldn't do any good. There's no evidence of breaking and entering, and they didn't actually take anything." He frowned darkly. "Must have been those teen-agers, just trying to scare me. They'll find out that I don't scare so easy. Not easy at all."

He chewed thoughtfully for a minute and then began to tell Aunt Laura about the house he was going to build in Arizona.

When Mr. Stafford finally left, Connie's mother went into action. She called Connie and Dan into the kitchen. "It's a beautiful sunny day, and I want to finish up my painting. Let's get all the chores over with this morning, okay?" She started to walk out of the kitchen and stopped with a hand on the doorknob. "Oh, I forgot about supper."

"We could put something in the Crockpot," Connie suggested. "And I'll make dessert, so you won't have to worry about it."

Her mother hugged her. "Thank you, honey. I'm going to spend the whole afternoon in the marsh."

Connie had been wanting to go down to see Stella in the photo blind, so she worked as quickly as possible through her piano practice and the other things that had to be done. Dan helped too, intent on some project of his own, and they finished in time for an early lunch. After they had eaten, her mother asked Dan to do his studying in the living room, where he would be handy if Aunt Laura should call.

At last Connie and her mother could start down the path to the marsh. Connie took her camera, her notebook, and a small folding chair for her mother, who had all her painting equipment to carry. When they reached the bluff, they stood there for a minute with the wind whipping the hair across their faces.

"Look how the sunshine turns the marsh to gold," her mother exclaimed. "Oh, this is such a lovely place!"

Connie agreed wholeheartedly. The wind was cold, but she liked the way it ruffled the ponds with brilliant blue and danced through the tawny plumes of the marsh grass. She helped her mother get set up in a protected place below the bluff before she hurried on toward the photo blind.

Stella's directions were easy to follow, and it was a good thing she had them, for the path would have been easy to miss. It began as a gap in the roadside weeds and then led through pines mixed with holly trees that towered far above her head. She'd never seen hollies like these. They had long, bare, knobby limbs that reached up to the light, and their prickly green leaves mingled with the topmost pine branches to make a dark canopy that shut out the sunny day.

Connie followed the faint trail as best she could, feeling more confident as soon as she saw water glimmering ahead of her. All at once she was there.

The photo blind was just a rough little hut built of dark, weathered wood. The way it snuggled into the tall grass at the edge of a pond, it seemed as much a part of the marsh as the overhanging trees.

She peered through the open space that served for a doorway. Stella was crouched over her camera at one of several small cutouts in the wall.

She greeted Connie with a smile and a finger to her lips, then motioned her over to the low window. Connie joined her quickly. A tall, grey-blue bird was stalking through the shallows right in front of them, his long thin legs moving like yellow stilts.

"Heron," whispered Stella. Her camera clicked as he speared a fish. A minute later the heron unfolded enormous wings and rose into the air.

Stella straightened up with a satisfied look on her face. "I love to watch herons."

"Do you think we'll see any swans?" Connie asked hopefully.

"Could be," said Stella. "There's a pair around here somewhere, and they often use this pond. We'll have to wait and see."

Today Stella's earrings were little silver ducks, and they flashed in the light as she swung her arms in a long stretch. "Photography is fun, but sometimes it takes a while to get a good shot," she said with a yawn. "Especially when you need a certain kind of picture."

As the afternoon wore on, Connie understood better what she meant. It seemed to take forever for Stella to get her camera focused and take a shot. Or she would take six different pictures of the same bird, changing something on her camera each time. The hut sheltered them from the tugging wind, but cold drafts swirled across the floor to numb Connie's fingers and toes.

Every once in a while a different kind of duck swam by, and Connie could stretch her cramped legs as she moved from one cutout to the next, watching. She took a few pictures, but she wanted to save most of her roll for the swans, if they ever came. Copying Stella, she noted each picture in her small red notebook.

Between pictures they talked in low voices. Connie mentioned her promise to make dessert for supper, and Stella offered to help her with a cake. Considering the way her last cake had turned out, Connie thought that was a wonderful idea. When Stella started talking about her two older brothers, she began to feel that they had something in common.

"Did they ever make you feel like a little kid?" she asked wistfully.

Stella nodded, as if she understood. "It seemed like they grew up all of a sudden and left me behind."

She bent to change a lens on her camera. "I was so proud of those big brothers of mine," she continued. "Sam played basketball, and Josh was a musician—he sang and could play a guitar as well as three other instruments. Sometimes Dad told visitors, 'Sam's got the muscles, and Josh's got the brains, and Stella—well, I guess she's got the looks in this family.' Then I'd run off and cry, because I wanted to have brains too."

"But you do," protested Connie. "You write stuff and you take pictures for important magazines."

Stella shook her head. "Back then I didn't know I was going to be a photographer. I didn't feel like I could do anything."

"Me too," murmured Connie. She sat down on the rough wooden floor and tucked her feet under her to keep warm.

Stella smiled. "My old grandma, she kept telling me, 'Now, chile, doan you go gettin' impatient with God's plan. You keep on doin' what you know is right.' Then she'd wave her cane at me and nod her wise old head and say, 'I reckon He's got somethin' special for my Stella—you just gotta ask Him 'bout it, and He'll show you when He's good an' ready.' "

Stella stopped to take a box of film out of her camera bag, and then she added, "So I learned a little about waiting for God, and I prayed a lot about it. After a while, He showed me what He wanted me to do. And He's not finished with me yet, I hope."

Connie watched Stella load her camera with fresh film and silently savored this new idea. It would be nice to know that God had something special for her, too. She wasn't so sure that she really wanted to be a photographer, after all. It was freezing in here and sort of boring between pictures.

Stella looked up from her camera. "Well, here they come at last," she said quietly.

Connie scrambled to her feet. "The swans!"

There were two of them. They were paddling slowly across the pond, necks held in a graceful curve and white feathers glistening against the blue water. They looked as lovely as any picture Connie had ever seen.

"Come on closer, you beauties," urged Stella in a whisper. "I'm glad they're mute swans," she told Connie. "They're the prettiest ones."

"How do you know what kind they are?" asked Connie.

"You can tell by the *S* curve of their necks; the other kinds of swans hold their necks straight. If you get a chance, look for the black knob at the base of their bills."

The swans stopped to feed, one dipping into the pond while the other surveyed the shore with a watchful eye. Stella's camera clicked, then clicked again, and Connie began taking pictures too.

After a few minutes, the pair resumed their leisurely swim. Gradually they drew closer, breasting the ripples with effortless grace, and Connie watched them in fascination. At last they reached the shore in front of the photo blind.

As they rooted there in the shallow water, Connie could see their round brown eyes and every detail of their brilliant white plumage. Sure enough, each one had a black knob at the base of its orange bill.

I could almost reach out and touch them, she thought.

Stella was taking one picture after another, and Connie followed her example, holding her camera as steady as she could and trying not to rush. It kept her busy until the swans finally drifted off in silent splendor.

When they were out of sight, she exchanged a smile with Stella. "Well, I used up all my film."

"How'd you like them?" Stella asked.

"They're beautiful," Connie said simply, "just like I'd always imagined."

Stella smiled, as if she thought so too. "I just wish they had paid us a longer visit. I need some more close-ups. Oh, look—the mallards."

A family of mallard ducks paddled by in formation, like a convoy of tiny ships. Connie stayed for a while longer, listening to them quack busily to each other, but after they were gone, she decided to leave too.

On her way back through the holly woods, she thought about Stella and the way she had prayed about God's plan for her life. Aunt Laura, too, had said that God had a plan for Christians. That was good to know. Somehow it gave her a feeling of confidence.

But what about now?

I don't know about the rest of my life, she thought, but I sure do want to win that photo contest.

It seemed strange to pray about something like that. She was used to praying for missionaries or for someone who had been in a car accident: important things. But this was important to her, wasn't it? And she'd heard Aunt Laura pray about all kinds of things.

She scuffed a foot through the dark brown pine needles on the path and began, hesitantly, to talk to Him. First she told Him how badly she wanted to win the contest. Then, once she had started, she couldn't stop. She told Him about Dan—how she was always doing dumb things when he was around and how worried she was that she might never be any good at anything. And then she asked Him to show her if He had something special for her to do.

By the time she finished, she was surprised to find that she had reached the end of the path. She stepped through the tall weeds with a lightened heart and ran down the road, swinging her camera.

When she reached the top of the bluff, she saw that Ricky stood there, half-hidden in the shadows of the pine trees. He seemed to be watching someone in the marsh.

Chapter Ten
Searching the Study

Connie joined Ricky, and right away she recognized the figure at the easel. "That's my mother," she told him proudly.

"What's she doing?"

"She's painting." From the look on his face, she could tell that he thought it was a strange thing to do. "She's an artist," Connie explained. "She paints pictures and then people buy them."

Ricky gave her a sideways glance and changed the subject abruptly. "I know a guy who can help you with your school project—he goes to college. He's practicing to be some kind of scientist, I think."

"Where does he live?" asked Connie, wondering at Ricky's sudden helpfulness.

"I don't know, but he's over that way, in the marsh." Ricky pointed away from the bird refuge. "Not very far—I can show you."

Connie shaded her eyes to look at the sun, slipping now toward the horizon. Mother was still painting, and Stella hadn't come up from the photo blind yet. "Okay. I'm supposed to make a cake for dessert, so I've got to hurry, but I guess I'll have time."

Ricky started down the path ahead of her. "Do you do that a lot?" he asked over his shoulder.

"Do what?" asked Connie, puzzled as much by the sound of longing in his voice as by his question.

"Bake cakes."

"Oh, that. No, I'm not a very good cook. It'll probably turn out terrible."

"Huh." He didn't say any more until they had passed Aunt Laura's house and reached the edge of Deer Meadow. "This way." He turned onto a narrow path that Connie hadn't noticed before. It seemed to wander aimlessly in slow curves through the woods, but the trees thinned at last, and she saw the edge of the salt marsh.

A young man sat on a rock beside the water, staring at the outgoing tide. As they approached, he pulled a notebook from his pocket.

"Hello, kids," he said pleasantly enough. He had a tanned face, dark eyes, and curly black hair that stuck out from under his blue cap.

Something about the flash of his eyes and the set of his cap, pulled down hard over his untidy hair, reminded Connie of a picture she'd once seen of a pirate. She stared at him with interest.

"Hi," said Ricky in his abrupt way. "Tell her what you're working on, like you told me."

It seemed to Connie that the man did not especially want to talk about anything, but he rubbed at his nose, which was rather too small and pointed to belong to a pirate, and began, "I'm a college student and I'm doing some research on the marsh grass around here. Specifically, *Spartina alterniflora* and *Spartina patens*."

He gestured vaguely at the tall grass that grew along the water. "The unusual thing about the *Spartinas* is their ability to thrive in a salt marsh, where their roots are submerged in salty water and the tides come in twice a day to cover the leaves as well."

He darted a quick glance at Connie, who had given up entirely on the idea of a pirate. "The *Spartinas* are dominant because of their special adaptation to the wetlands. And they're an important part of the food chain, you understand."

"Umm," said Connie, not sure that she understood at all.

"She's studying too," Rick supplied helpfully. "About feathers."

"Well, that's interesting," the man said. But he didn't sound very interested. "My name's Hank. What's yours?"

After telling him, Connie explained, "I don't really live here. We're just visiting Laura Hendrick. She lives in that house up on the hill." Connie waved in the direction from which they had come.

Suddenly she remembered the cake. "Oh, it's getting late. I'd better go."

"Me too," spoke up Ricky.

The man nodded, hunching himself into his gray jacket as though he were cold. "See you later," he called as they hurried into the woods.

"He was kind of nice," said Connie, walking as fast as she could, "although he sounded as if he were reading out of a book instead of talking. But maybe college students get that way." When they reached Deer Meadow, she said, "I've got to run now, Ricky."

"Okay, make a good cake," he said with a grin, and Connie was surprised that he had remembered.

When she rushed into the kitchen, Stella was already there, leafing through a cookbook. "Sorry I'm late," Connie told her breathlessly. "Don't worry, I just got here too," Stella murmured. "I sure hope there's a cake mix in the cupboards somewhere. These recipes look fearsome." Connie giggled. "I saw a couple of cake mixes yesterday." She opened a cabinet door. "Here they are. What kind do you want?"

"What's Dan's favorite? Why don't we make that?"

"Okay," said Connie. "It'll be chocolate, then."

Before long the cake was baking in the oven. Connie had almost finished beating the icing when Dan poked his head into the kitchen. "Sure smells good in here. What's going on?"

"A cake," Connie told him proudly. "We made it for supper."

Dan screwed up his face. "*You* made a cake? Oh, no—" He staggered out, making awful gagging sounds.

Connie started after him with a sharp reply, but the sound of Stella's laughter stopped her.

"Just like my brother, Sam," she told Connie with a grin. "Reckon those could have been his very words. Brothers are all the same." Connie had to grin too, and her irritation faded.

Stella called, "Hey, Dan, come back here a minute. I want to ask you two something."

When Dan had stumbled back into the kitchen, still pretending to look sick, Stella said, "I'm going to rent an airplane Saturday morning, to fly over the bird refuge. Would either of you like to come along?"

"Sure!" exclaimed Dan, straightening up.

"Me too," Connie said. "Why are you doing it?"

"I need some aerial photos for my project, and I like to fly every once in a while to keep my license current," Stella explained.

"What about Ricky?" asked Connie. "Would there be room for him too?"

"That's a good idea." Stella cocked her head to think about it. "He sure doesn't weigh much, and the airplane has four seats. Why don't you find out if he'd like to come?"

When the cake was finished, Connie served it for dessert, feeling satisfied with the results. Even though Dan didn't actually say it was good, he asked for a second piece, and she knew what that meant.

While she was putting the leftovers away, she remembered how interested Ricky had been in the cake and decided to keep a slice for him. Carefully she wrapped it up and slipped it into a corner of the refrigerator, wondering about him. At first she'd thought he might have run away from home; he was so ragged. But perhaps not. If Stella was right, and he did live around here, maybe she could get to know him better.

After supper when Connie told Aunt Laura about visiting the photo blind and finally seeing the swans, her aunt looked pleased. "Good for you!" she exclaimed. "Aren't they lovely?"

"I've never been that close to anything so wild and beautiful," Connie said.

"I know what you mean—it's a thrill," Aunt Laura agreed. "I've spent quite a bit of time in that photo blind myself."

She gave Connie a twinkling smile. "I always used to be in such a hurry that I missed a lot. Back then,

I never would've had the patience to watch and wait for those swans. I'm glad you got to see them."

She looked past Connie to the living room. "Oh, there's Dan. Would you catch him for me?"

When Dan came into her bedroom, she asked, "Are you going to get out your telescope tonight? It's nice and clear."

"I don't know. I can't see past the trees in the right direction. Maybe I'll have to forget about Jupiter's moons."

He sounded so disheartened that Connie felt sorry for him. "What if you set up your telescope on the platform of the Lookout Tree?" she asked.

Dan's face brightened. "Wouldn't hurt to try."

"I'll help you carry your stuff," she offered.

"Okay," he agreed without enthusiasm, and Connie knew he was remembering the other times she'd meant to help him and had dropped something.

"Not tonight," she promised herself as she carried his telescope tripod down the stairs.

On the way to Deer Meadow, Dan asked, "Who's this Ricky you and Stella were talking about?"

"He's a kid I ran into when I was down in the marsh." Then Connie told him everything she could about Ricky.

When she finished, Dan asked, "He's probably not saved, is he?"

"No, I guess not," Connie said slowly.

"Remember those meetings we had last month at church?" Dan said in a low voice. "Well, I decided that I'm going to try and be a better witness. Maybe I'll get a chance to talk to Ricky about the Lord."

Connie thought about that. Dan had memorized a lot of Bible verses, and he'd probably be good at explaining the plan of salvation, but she couldn't help wondering how Ricky would react.

At the Lookout Tree, she took her time hoisting the tripod up to the platform, so she wouldn't bang it. Then, while Dan set up his telescope, she leaned against the railing and looked up at the sky. It was deep black, filled with more stars than she had ever seen before. They were so bright that even Dan ought to be satisfied. He must be, for he was whistling the way he always did when he was happy.

As she turned toward the sea, she felt the bite of the wind, cold and tangy with salt, and she thrust her hands deep into her jacket pockets. From here she could see all the way to the horizon, where a jeweled string of lights marked the shoreline of Atlantic City.

"I got it!" Dan exclaimed. "That's Jupiter. Where's my notebook?"

Connie handed it to him and watched him make a careful sketch, wondering if she'd ever know as much as he did.

Far off to their right, a flickering light suddenly blossomed, like a strange orange flower in the darkness. "Dan," she whispered, "what's that?"

He looked up from his notebook. "Some kind of fire, maybe." As he spoke, a series of staccato explosions ripped into the still night.

"Guns?" cried Connie.

"We'd better find out," Dan said. "That's over in the bird refuge. Help me get this thing down, will you? I can't leave it here."

They struggled down the ladder with the unwieldy telescope and tripod and hurried back through the woods.

As Dan set his equipment inside the porch door, Stella ran out of the house, pulling on her jacket. "You heard it too?" Not waiting for an answer, she plunged down the path to the marsh.

Connie followed her as fast as she could, stumbling in the darkness, with Dan right behind her. The night air seemed to be filled with the rat-tat-tat of machine gun fire. Stella led them past the bluff and through more woods to a clearing that opened out above the grassy hill where the Canada geese fed.

Its far side was lit by the leaping flames of a bonfire, and around it milled half a dozen dark figures. One of them picked up something and hurled it toward the pools beside the dike, and another explosion shattered the night. The group at the fire erupted into mocking laughter.

"Kids!" muttered Stella.

The wail of a siren sliced through the next explosion, and a police car, lights flashing, screeched onto the road beside the hill. Instantly the dark figures melted into the shadows.

Two policemen jumped out of the car and one of them ran to the bonfire. He looked it over for a second, turned his back to it, and spoke through a bullhorn. "Now you kids listen to me. Those firecrackers you're throwing are illegal. Besides that, you're trespassing on government land. This is the only warning you'll get. Next time, I'll arrest the whole bunch of you."

His voice rose above the tumult of bird cries, and there was no answer from the shadows. He turned to his companion and they began dousing the fire.

Connie whispered to Stella, "Do you think those are the teen-agers Mr. Stafford was talking about?"

"Could be," she answered. "He's probably the one who called the police. It's a good thing they got here right away."

Slowly they retraced their steps to Aunt Laura's house. "How could firecrackers make that terrible noise?" Connie asked. "It sounded like they were shooting off guns out here."

Dan said, "They probably used cherry bombs. If you set them off inside tin cans, it sounds pretty loud."

Later that evening, Connie was careful to pull the draperies tightly closed, and she checked to make sure that her doors and windows were all locked. If she listened hard enough, it seemed that she could still hear the teens' raucous laughter.

She wondered if Mr. Stafford was right about one of them being a burglar. She hoped not. But the only other person she could think of was the man from Atlantic City who wanted to buy Aunt Laura's land. Connie didn't like that idea either—it was too scary.

Even worse was remembering that whoever he was, he already knew his way around the inside of this house.

No, she wouldn't think about that; she'd think about the missing shell. Tonight she'd search through the rest of the drawers of shells. And after that, she'd finish the book she had been reading—there were only two chapters left.

As soon as she came down for breakfast the next morning, Connie could tell that her mother was in a house-cleaning mood. The furniture in the living room had been pulled to the center, and Aunt Laura's old upright vacuum cleaner stood there, poised for action.

Breakfast was a quick affair of cold cereal, and Connie had time for only a short talk with Aunt Laura before her mother called her to help. Meanwhile, she found out what had started this flurry of cleaning. Mrs. Atkins and several other ladies from the church were coming to visit on Sunday afternoon.

"As soon as you've done the dishes, pile the kitchen chairs on the table and we'll do the floor," Mother directed. "Dan, you can start on the living room rug."

Reluctantly Connie put off her own plans for the morning. Mother didn't get this way very often, but the whole family had to work hard while it lasted. At least she wasn't the kind of mother who made a career out of house cleaning.

"Your Aunt Mabel phoned last night." Mother paused on her way out the door with an armful of rugs.

"What for?"

"Just to find out how things are going, that's all. And to remind us that she'll be here next Friday."

Mother didn't sound very happy at the prospect of Aunt Mabel's visit, and her words reminded Connie that she had less than a week left. If Aunt Laura could make arrangements for the house the way she wanted to, then Aunt Mabel wouldn't have any reason for suggesting a nursing home.

"I've got to find that shell," Connie told herself.

She thought about it while she pushed the sponge mop back and forth across the kitchen floor. Last night she had finished looking through the drawers of shells. The only thing left was to search the rest of the study. If only she could find the missing diary!

As soon as her work was done, Connie hurried upstairs to the study. In order to reach the topmost books, she used a small, wooden step stool that she'd found in a corner. She read the book titles with interest as she went, stopping every once in a while to pull out a book and browse through its pages.

On the highest shelf above the desk she found an interesting-looking pair of books about seashells. She took down the first thick volume and scanned its table of contents. Good, there was a whole chapter on cowries—in the second volume.

As she started to slide the book back into place, she saw that something was wedged behind the second volume. Triumphantly she pulled out a small green book. Yes, the date showed that this was the missing diary. But what an odd place to keep it!

She heard footsteps in the hall and remembered that Dan had been planning to get more books from the study. She had to read this diary without being disturbed. Quickly she slipped back through the wall to her room. A glance at the clock assured her that she still had a little time before lunch, so she stretched out across the bed and opened the diary expectantly.

Chapter Eleven
The Diary Puzzle

The diary began where the other one left off, at the first week of October. Once again Connie found pages that were filled with endless details about bird sightings, all in Philip Hendrick's tiny, neat handwriting. By the time she got to the entries for the middle of October, she was beginning to feel discouraged. But then, right after a notation about a green-winged teal, she found:

Will hide gc until I decide what to do. Get it out of here.

Next came a statement that didn't make very much sense. *My dear Laura, remember the Christmas swans.* It was followed by a short paragraph that sounded different from everything else she had read. Although it was written in the same compact form as the rest of the diary, it seemed that Philip Hendrick was trying out a new writing style.

She gave the paragraph a curious glance—it said something about the morning mist and the marsh—and returned to the sentence that was clearly meant for Aunt Laura. After puzzling over it for a minute, she went on.

A short time later, on a page dated near the end of October, she discovered another cryptic comment: *Some shells gone. Found Tatum in here again and fired him.*

Philip Hendrick had been right in deciding to hide the golden cowrie, Connie thought. And it was good to know that Tatum, whoever he was, had been fired. She searched through the rest of the diary, right to where it ended with the January 10 entry, but found nothing else of interest. She sat staring dreamily at it until Dan yelled up the stairs: "Connie—lunch."

"Okay, coming," she called back. She slid off the bed with a feeling of accomplishment. Plowing through all that small print had been worth it. She made a quick trip to put the diary back into its place in the set. Now she had a real mystery to work on. Maybe this afternoon she'd go down to the marsh; it seemed like a good place for thinking.

After lunch, when she ran up to her room to get her jacket, Connie glimpsed a young raccoon climbing one of the trees outside. Ricky must be there with Coon, and whether he'd admit it or not, he was probably waiting for her to come out. She hurried to meet him, remembering at the last minute to take the package of cake she had saved.

He stood near the pine trees, just as she had expected, but his back was to the house, and he appeared to be watching his raccoon in the tree.

"Hi," she said.

He swung around, his face more friendly than she'd ever seen it. She handed him the cake. "Here's a piece of that cake we made. See if you like it."

He gave her a surprised glance but didn't hesitate to peel off the wrapping and take a big bite. Dark crumbs scattered down the front of his jacket. With a lopsided grin, he mumbled, "It's good. Did you make it all by yourself?"

"No, Stella helped me. Remember, you met her?" Connie said. "She's probably down at the marsh now. Let's see if we can find her."

Ricky followed Connie silently. She looked back once and saw that he was licking the last of the icing from his fingers while Coon rode on his shoulder.

When they reached the bluff, Connie stopped, as she always did, to survey the marsh. She caught sight of a large bird, far on the horizon, heading in toward them. It flew low over the water with laboring wing-beats that looked awkward even to her inexperienced eyes. She pointed wordlessly, but Ricky was already watching it.

As the bird drew closer to shore, she recognized the black head and neck of a Canada goose. "What's the matter with him?" she asked.

"Looks like his flight feathers got shot off one side," Ricky said, his eyes intent.

It seemed to Connie that she could feel the desperation that drove the injured bird onward, one slow wing-beat after another. "Come on, you can do it," she murmured.

"He knows he'll be safe here until he grows new feathers," Ricky added suddenly. "That's what I like about this place."

The goose struggled on toward the refuge, finally crossing the dikes and gliding down onto a pond, out of sight.

Connie let out the breath she had been holding. "He made it," she said. "I'm glad."

"Yeah, me too." Ricky gave her a quick grin and slid over the edge of the bluff.

When they found Stella, she was standing near the resident flock of Canada geese, talking to a blond young man in a gray uniform. Connie decided that he was probably one of the rangers who worked at the bird refuge. They must have been discussing the wild dog, because Stella motioned toward Connie and Ricky as they came by. "Those two had to climb a tree to get away from that dog."

"Yes, we'll have to do something about it," the ranger said. "Feral dogs are a real menace to our birds." He turned to leave and then added, "Tell Mrs. Hendrick not to worry about the young ruffians who've been bothering us lately. The police said they'll patrol this whole area pretty closely for a while. Tom Frost was out here today, checking around, and he'll be back tonight with a couple of his men."

"Thank you. She'll be happy to hear that," Stella said.

After the man had gone, she smiled at Connie and Ricky. "Reckon I'll go and roost in the photo blind for a while and see if those swans will cooperate for some close-ups. Connie, I noticed some feathers on the other side of the hill. Do you need any for your collection?"

"I sure do." Connie looked at Ricky. "Want to help me look?"

"Yeah," he said. Without waiting for her, he trotted off over the crest of the hill, as though he were suddenly very interested in feathers.

Stella's dark eyes followed him. "For some reason, I think that boy doesn't like me. I'm glad you can be a friend to him, anyway." She gave Connie a warm glance of approval. "You'll have to hurry if you're going to catch up with him."

Connie was happy to find a white feather that Ricky told her came from a snow goose, as well as three more Canada goose feathers in different shades of brown. While they strolled back along the muddy edge of a marsh pond, they talked about her feather collection and the other things that Connie had to do for school.

Ricky said, "Wish I could go to school that way. I hate the stuff they make us learn."

"Well, at least you have the day off today," Connie pointed out. "Is it some kind of holiday?"

He looked uncomfortable. "Nope—I just took off."

"Won't you get into trouble?"

"Not if nobody finds out," Ricky said shortly. "You going to be around tomorrow?"

That reminded Connie of what she'd been going to ask him. "I'm going for an airplane ride in the morning." At the look of amazement on his face, she quickly added, "You can come too, Stella said. She's going to fly over the marsh and take some pictures."

His face went blank. "Uh-uh. Not with her." He threw a sideways glance at Connie. "Somethin' about her scares me. She sort of looks right through a guy."

Connie rather liked Stella's clear, direct gaze, but she said nothing. Ricky bent to pick up a muddy clam shell that a gull had dropped. He held it out to her. "Are you going to collect shells too?"

She looked at the chipped shell and took it from him reluctantly. "I don't think so. I haven't seen very many good ones around here."

"Your uncle had a lot of them, didn't he?"

"Yes, but they mostly came from friends who are missionaries."

While she was wondering how Ricky knew about Philip Hendrick's shell collection, he muttered, "Who'd want to be a missionary, anyway?"

Connie swallowed a gulp of surprise. "If it weren't for missionaries, a lot of people wouldn't know about God."

He kicked at a thick clump of marsh grass as he passed it. "What's so great about God?"

I sure wish Dan were here, Connie thought. "Well, God loves us," she began carefully. "And—"

"Huh," Ricky interrupted. "You can't prove that."

"The Bible says so." Connie knew there was a good verse somewhere about God's love, but she couldn't remember exactly what it was.

By this time they had reached Aunt Laura's house and Ricky turned away, saying gruffly, "Maybe I'll see you tomorrow." He let out a shrill whistle, and Coon scuttled out of the bushes to climb quickly onto Ricky's shoulder.

Connie watched them go, wishing she had done a better job of talking to Ricky about the Lord. "Maybe I'll get another chance," she told herself hopefully.

She carried her feathers upstairs to add to her collection, and then, remembering the wounded goose, wrote a whole page about it in her journal.

When she finished, she took the green diary downstairs to show Aunt Laura. But her mother warned her that Aunt Laura wasn't feeling well and would be going to bed early. "I'll just stay a minute," Connie promised.

Quickly she told Aunt Laura about finding the diary. "It sounds as if your husband hid the golden cowrie somewhere, and I think he left you some clues, but I don't understand them." She pointed out the puzzling passage.

Aunt Laura leaned forward to peer at the small book. Then she shook her head wearily. "I can't read that tiny writing anymore." After a moment she suggested, "Why don't you copy it out for me in nice big letters? Then we can look at it together. Okay?"

"Okay." Impulsively Connie leaned over and kissed Aunt Laura's soft cheek. "I'm really praying about our secret," she whispered. "I just know the Lord's going to do something special, so you've got to get well fast."

"Thank you, Connie," Aunt Laura whispered back. And then she chuckled softly. "I'm so glad He sent you here."

By the end of the evening, however, Connie felt her confidence slipping away. She had decided to tackle the odd little paragraph on her own, and she'd set to work with high hopes. So Philip Hendrick liked puzzles? She did too. In fact, she and Dan had spent all one summer making up secret messages for each other to decode. There must be some trick to this one.

She had tried every code she could think of, but all she came up with was meaningless gibberish like *mshhd hmrh timrig*. Finally, when her brain felt numb, she copied out the paragraph for Aunt Laura. With a sigh, she returned the diary to its place in the study. Maybe, once Aunt Laura read it, she'd be able to figure out what it meant.

The next morning, however, there was no time for them to have their usual talk. Stella wanted to get an early start to the airport because cloudy weather was predicted for the afternoon. And since Mr. Stafford was coming over to see Aunt Laura while they were gone, there was a batch of cookies to bake. Mother had an absent-minded look on her face that meant she was thinking about a painting, so she would probably spend some time down in the marsh while Mr. Stafford was visiting with Aunt Laura.

The airport was not the big, busy place that Connie had pictured. It had a small orange windsock ballooning importantly from a flagpole, and its only runway was a long strip of concrete in the middle of a pasture. They parked next to a narrow white building that squatted at one end of the runway, and Stella went inside to finish making arrangements for the airplane.

In just a few minutes, she was back. "All set now. Got your cameras?" She led the way to a trim red and white airplane on the concrete ramp and showed them how to step up into the cockpit. She piled her camera equipment in the front seat beside her, and Connie and Dan took the back seat.

After Stella had finished a careful preflight check of the plane, she made sure they had their seat belts on. Then she handed each of them a pack of gum. "Try chewing it if your ears bother you," she advised.

Soon they were taxiing down the runway, bumping over the seams in the concrete as they went. Connie watched the tall grass and weeds slipping past, and the roar of the engine filled her ears.

They went faster and faster until suddenly the bumping was gone, and she felt the smooth lift of air beneath the plane. Connie sat very still, staring at the blue sky all around and feeling a slow excitement creep through her. For several minutes, the little plane climbed steadily, gaining altitude, and her ears began to pop. Dan tapped

the pack of gum in her hand. Hurriedly she unwrapped a couple of sticks and chewed them up while she pressed her face against the window to look out.

They had stopped climbing, and the plane was beginning a long, curving turn across the marsh. Below them lay countless winter-brown hummocks and islands set in a background of glittering dark water. As Stella dropped the plane lower, Connie could make out the trees fringing the shore and the fuzzy, brown marsh grass.

Stella said something to them, pointing out the window, and soon Connie recognized the long, narrow lines of the dikes in the bird refuge. The flocks of snow geese looked like small rafts of shining white, bobbing on the larger ponds. As the plane glided along, Stella began taking pictures.

Connie reached for her own camera. When she returned to the window, she noticed an animal half-hidden in the underbrush at one end of a pond. She poked at Dan to get his attention and moved over so he could see it too. As they watched, the animal sprang into full view and snatched at a lone dot of white near the shore.

Chapter Twelve
Danger in the Marsh

"Oh, no!" Connie cried. "It's the wolf—I mean that dog—he's caught a snow goose."

Stella must have seen it too, for she banked the plane into a sharp, plunging turn that took Connie's breath away. But now they could see the dog clearly. It lifted a great shaggy head as the plane swung past, and Connie groaned aloud at the sight of the still, white form under its feet. Just in time, she remembered to take a picture.

The plane leveled out and slowly began to climb as it passed over Aunt Laura's house. Dan pointed down to it, and Connie took a quick picture, then watched in fascination as the Lookout Tree and Deer Meadow slid by. A short distance into the woods she could see the small brown roof of a cabin. She peered through bare-limbed trees at the two men who stood in front of it. One of them wore something blue on his head, and the other had a plump figure and a green coat that looked familiar.

At her shoulder, Dan said "Stafford," and she nodded, recognizing him. He was turning away from the other man now, walking back toward Aunt Laura's house. The plane's wings slanted as it rose higher, and Connie lost sight of him.

Once again they glided over the bird refuge in a long slow pass, and Stella took picture after picture. The dog was gone, but Connie thought she could still see something white on the ground. "Why didn't the goose fly away?" she cried to Dan.

Stella motioned to them from the front seat, and Connie leaned forward so she could hear above the roar of the engine. "That goose wasn't out in the open water with the flock, so it must have been sick or lame—that's the kind of bird the dog would go after."

Connie sat back against the seat with an indignant thump. "Well, I sure hope someone does something about that dog—soon."

Stella nodded vigorously and turned back to finish taking her pictures. Dan raised his camera for one of his careful shots, and Connie took a few more pictures too, hoping that some of them would turn out. All too soon, Stella began to guide the plane back down to the airport.

"Ricky would have loved this," Connie remarked as they taxied over to the hangar. "And if he had come, you might've had a chance to say something to him," she told Dan. "I don't think he goes to church or anything." She described their conversation about missionaries.

He was putting his camera back into its case, but he listened intently. After a moment's thought, he said, "John 3:16 is a good verse about God's love."

"Oh, I know that one," Connie exclaimed. "I just wish I had remembered it."

"I've got to talk to him," Dan said, half to himself.

The plane rolled to a halt and Connie crawled out of it, following Dan. As they stood beside the plane, Stella glanced at the clouds that were piling up on the horizon. "Good thing we got our pictures this morning. That reminds me—those rolls of film I brought in should be ready now. We'll stop by on our way through town."

Usually when Connie went to pick up her pictures, she stood right there in the drug store and looked at them. But this time, when Stella handed her the fat white envelope, she slipped it under one arm to keep until she got home. That's what Stella had done with hers, only she'd had five envelopes. Besides, Connie didn't especially want Dan looking over her shoulder when she opened them, saying "What's that supposed to be?"

She had to wait longer than she thought, because they ate lunch at a hamburger place and then did some grocery shopping on the way home. But as soon as she was back in her bedroom, she opened the envelope.

Good thing I waited, she thought, frowning at them. Some of the pictures seemed to be of nothing in particular—she'd have to check her notebook—and three were badly blurred. There were a few, though, that she might be able to use. She could put them into her journal or even make a special album.

But now, before it got too late, she wanted to go down to the marsh to see if she could find the place where the dog had attacked the snow goose. Stella was probably down there already.

When Connie reached the bluff, she met Ricky coming up the slope. Coon was riding on his shoulder, nibbling daintily at an apple core. Ricky wore an eager expression, as if he had been looking for her, but all he said was, "Hi."

"Hi yourself." When he didn't answer, Connie tried, "Sure looks like it's going to rain."

He stopped beside her to look back at the marsh. Heavy clouds hung low over the water, and mist was already blurring the horizon. Abruptly he asked, "Remember you were telling me about your uncle's shell collection? Have you ever seen it?"

"Sure," answered Connie. "He's got a little room with drawers and drawers full of shells." She thought about all the time she had spent searching through those drawers for the golden cowrie, and she sighed.

"Does he have any rare shells?" persisted Ricky.

"I guess so," she answered cautiously. She wondered if she should tell him about the missing cowrie. "Some of them are really pretty—" She broke off as a dark-haired man appeared among the pine trees a short distance from where they stood.

It was Hank, the college student. He must have walked up from the woods, but he had slipped so silently, so smoothly through the trees that she hadn't heard him coming.

He wore the same grey jacket and light blue cap that he'd had on the other day. She gazed at his cap. From the airplane she'd seen someone wearing a knitted cap like that. It must have been Hank. Maybe he even lived in that little brown house.

She wanted to ask Ricky about it, but Hank was passing them now, murmuring a polite greeting. Ricky watched him go, then mumbled, "See you later," and hurried down the path after him, as if he had suddenly remembered something important.

Connie shrugged and glanced again at the sky. The way those clouds looked, she'd better go on down to the marsh before it started to rain.

After considerable searching, she came across a tangle of dog tracks on the muddy edge of a pond. A few feathers, caught in a weedy thicket, were all that remained of the goose. Connie stared at them sadly, then chose a slender, white tail feather to keep for her collection. She stroked it gently as she wandered down the narrow road that led farther out along the dike.

Ahead of her, a trio of brown and white gulls were dropping clams on the road to break them open, swooping down with triumphant shrieks to steal morsels from each other. After she had watched their antics for a while, she reluctantly decided to start for home. If Mother had painted all afternoon, she'd be expecting some help with supper.

She had turned back, still listening to the gulls' squabbling cries, when she first heard the motorcycles. There were two of them, sleek and black. They came charging out of the woods like a pair of angry wild animals and swung onto the dike road with a suddenness that startled her.

She flinched as they roared past, sweeping perilously close and kicking up tiny sharp rocks as they went. The drivers wore helmets with black visors that covered their faces and made them look like strange, alien beings. One of them turned to stare back at her, and she began to walk faster.

As they thundered on down the dike, a cloud of snow geese rose with deafening cries of alarm and stormed over her head. Connie watched in sympathy as the frightened birds flew past.

A sudden blast of noise filled her ears. The cyclists had come back. They were almost upon her. She stepped aside, but not far enough. One of them was swerving, following her, as if he meant to run right over her. She leaped away from the cycle's hot breath and stumbled in the weeds. She felt her ankle turn under her, and then she was falling, sliding down the rocky shoulder of the dike. She rolled against a thick clump of grass and lay still, breathing hard and listening to the fading growl of the motorcycles. When she was sure they had gone, she tried to sit up. Pain stabbed at her ankle. She persisted, pulling herself to her knees.

One elbow was scratched and bleeding, and her shoulder hurt where she had fallen on it. But her ankle was the worst. When she tried to put her weight on it, pain streaked up her leg, making her sway dizzily. This sprain wasn't as bad as some she'd had, but there was no way she could walk on it. Carefully she eased back down to the ground. What should she do now?

"Lord, you can see me here," she whispered. "Please send someone to find me."

At least I can crawl, she thought, feeling encouraged. I've got to get back up to the road. Then I can yell for help.

She blinked back the silly tears that would only slow her down and worked her way up the side of the dike, through the weeds and stones, to the road. From there she called out, holding herself painfully upright for as long as she could, but her voice seemed to lose itself in the wide grey expanse of the marsh. Once she thought she heard an answering cry, but it was only a gull.

At last she let herself sprawl in the sand. She fell silent, rubbing at her ankle and wishing that it weren't getting dark so fast. What if that wild dog should happen to wander by, looking for another lame, injured creature? Would he . . . no! Determinedly she turned her back on the shadowy woods and faced out toward the marsh.

A minute later she heard a crunching sound and jerked around to see what it was. Someone—oh, good, it was Stella—was hurrying down the road toward her.

Chapter Thirteen
The Swans' Secret

Stella's dark face was creased with worry. "What's happened to you, child?"

The strong arm around her felt wonderfully warm, but Connie still shivered. "Those guys on the bikes—they came so close, I fell down the dike—" Just remembering made the tears threaten again.

"You mean the two motorcyclists? They tried to run you down?"

Connie nodded.

"Well, you don't have to worry 'bout them anymore," Stella said grimly. "They've already been caught. The police were waiting for them at the exit from the refuge. And the Lord had it all planned for me to be walking back by this road. Now let's see about getting you home."

It seemed like a long way, even with Stella supporting her. Once they reached the porch, Stella called Dan to help carry Connie into the living room, and Connie sank into the softness of the sofa with relief.

All Dan said was "What'd you do, sprain that ankle again?" But Mother hurried to get some ice, and then they moved her into Aunt Laura's bedroom so everyone could listen while Connie described what had happened.

"And I wasn't even doing anything to them," she finished indignantly. She shifted her legs, forgetting the ankle, and winced with pain.

"Those rats!" Dan muttered. "Good thing the police picked them up so fast."

Aunt Laura nodded in agreement. "Tom Frost—he's my policeman friend—told me that they've started patrolling the refuge pretty closely now."

Mother was gently examining Connie's ankle. She'd had plenty of experience with sprains, since Connie seemed to sprain an ankle at least once a year. Now she smiled up at Connie. "It doesn't look serious, but it's pretty swollen. Keep the ice pack on it."

Actually, it doesn't feel that bad, Connie thought. It's just the way it happened that makes it seem so horrible. And now I'll have to limp around everywhere for the next few days.

Dan had to help get supper ready, and while they ate, Mother remarked, "I wanted to bake a ton of cookies tonight because tomorrow is Sunday and those ladies are coming." She gave Connie a worried glance. "I don't know how I'm going to manage without you."

"I can mix stuff up," Connie pointed out. "And if we make drop cookies, I can do the dropping part."

"I'll measure things for you if I get a few fringe benefits, like licking the bowl," offered Dan with a grin.

Mother smiled and jumped up from the table. "Okay, we can do it! Free samples for everyone who helps." She opened a cupboard door and stared into it. "How about chocolate chip, peanut butter, and oatmeal-raisin?"

It was late when Connie finally got up to her room that evening. Mother had been extra particular about cleaning things up, since company was coming. Then she'd wrapped Connie's ankle in an elastic bandage, warned her to stay off it, and had Dan help her up the stairs.

Connie stretched out across her bed and yawned. Before all this happened, she'd planned to work on Philip Hendrick's puzzle again, just in case she'd missed something. But Mother would have a fit if she didn't stay in bed.

She sat up gingerly so she wouldn't bang her ankle. The paragraph she had copied out for Aunt Laura was right here on the bedside table, though. She'd look at that. If she could just figure it out, she had the feeling that it would tell what he had done with the shell.

She picked up the sheet of paper and read the paragraph through again. Then she studied the lists of words that she'd worked on last night. Take the first word of each line? The last word of each line? No matter how she arranged them, they didn't make sense.

Finally she put the paper down and tossed her crumpled notes into the wastebasket.

She began to get ready for bed, feeling slow and clumsy because of her ankle. It hurt every time she moved it, warning her that getting around in the marsh tomorrow was going to be a problem. Everything's gone wrong, she thought, suddenly disheartened. I can't even walk right. How am I ever going to get any good pictures for the contest?

The rain that had threatened all day splattered noisily against the window pane. It reminded her of what had happened in the marsh this afternoon and how the Lord had sent Stella to find her. She'd forgotten to thank Him for that.

As soon as she was back in bed, she turned her face into the pillow and began to pray. First she thanked the Lord for sending Stella, and then she just talked to Him. It was a comfort to tell Him how discouraged she was about everything: the contest, Aunt Laura's house, the shell, the puzzle.

Afterwards, she listened drowsily to the pattering rain, her mind still on the puzzle. That sentence beginning "My dear Laura" must be the key to the whole thing. Tomorrow she'd start all over again, after she'd talked to Aunt Laura.

The next morning before Dan came to help her downstairs, Connie slipped the paragraph for Aunt Laura into her pocket. She was glad she'd remembered to bring it when Dan told her that Aunt Laura had especially asked that Connie join her for breakfast.

Mother let her sit in the big chair next to Aunt Laura's bed, where she could prop up her ankle on a footstool. Connie settled back, feeling cozy. It was kind of fun watching Dan trot back and forth with the tray, although he didn't spill the cocoa like she sometimes did.

She made herself wait until Aunt Laura finished eating and had leaned back against the pillows with a second cup of cocoa. Then she took out the paper. "Here's the part of the diary that I copied out for you. I sure hope you can understand what it means."

Aunt Laura put on her glasses and read it silently. It seemed to take her a long time. At last she looked up at Connie with a puzzled expression. "This doesn't sound at all like the things Philip usually wrote in his journals."

"That's what I thought," Connie told her eagerly. "He said he was going to hide the shell, so I thought this might be some kind of a secret message because it's so different."

"You've tried taking every other word and all those kinds of codes?" asked Aunt Laura. "There's one he did once, where each word stood for a letter of the alphabet." She studied the paper for a minute, then gave it an impatient twitch. "No, that wouldn't work. I'm sorry, Connie. I just don't know what it means."

"But what about the Christmas swans?" asked Connie, trying to hide her disappointment.

"Well, he's probably referring to one of the bottles in my collection. I keep them on the window sills for the light to shine through."

Mother had already opened the curtains, and from where she sat, Connie could see the pair of glass bottles she had admired once before.

Aunt Laura went on, "I'm sure you've heard of the song called *The Twelve Days of Christmas.*" In a low voice she sang, "On the first day of Christmas, my true love gave to me. . . ." Then she smiled at Connie. "Philip gave me two glass bottles every Christmas for six years. Each bottle represented a different one of the days of Christmas."

She chuckled. "He told me later that he bought the whole set when it was on sale, then kept it hidden so I wouldn't find it while he was giving them to me. Pretty nice way to take care of your Christmas shopping, huh?"

Connie glanced back over at the green and rose-colored bottles. "I don't remember a swan on either of those. Where are the rest of them?"

"On the living room window sills. There's a white one for 'seven swans a-swimming.' It's made out of milk glass."

"That's right. Now I remember where they are." Connie leaned back to think, wishing she could get up and look at that white bottle. "I wonder how the swans could be connected with anything."

"The white one is a favorite of mine because of the swans," Aunt Laura said slowly. "I loved to watch them at the marsh—like you. But I don't see what it has to do with the shell, either."

"Seven swans a-swimming . . ." murmured Connie. "Maybe it's the number. Did he especially like *seven?*"

Aunt Laura shook her head. "I don't think so."

Connie's mother paused in the doorway. "Are you two finished talking? As soon as the dishes are done, we could listen to a sermon tape. We'd better do that while everything is still peaceful around here."

"That's a good idea." Aunt Laura smiled at Connie. "I'll keep thinking about those swans."

Connie puzzled over the white swans while she sat on a stool by the sink to dry the dishes, and she thought about them whenever she had a chance during the day. It turned out to be a busy one, just as Mother had predicted.

Connie helped as much as she could, mostly by sitting in the kitchen, getting refreshments ready. Her ankle felt better today and didn't bother her as long as she was careful not to put her full weight on it.

Of course, Mr. Stafford dropped in for a visit too, and for once he wasn't wearing his big fishing boots. Connie limped into the living room with a fresh plate of cookies, thinking that he always seemed to know when Mother had just finished baking.

He didn't stay long, though, once Mrs. Atkins arrived. He'd been sitting on the sofa, saying gallant things to all the ladies and telling his stories, when Mrs. Atkins marched briskly through the door.

She gazed pointedly at the cookie crumbs on his shirt front and gave him a chilly smile. She didn't really say anything unkind to him, not that Connie heard, but his round face took on a deflated look. It wasn't five minutes later that he was bowing himself out of the room, and Connie couldn't help feeling sorry for him. He must have done battle with Mrs. Atkins before and lost.

After the visitors had gone, Mother insisted that Connie rest her ankle for an hour, so she spent the time on the living room sofa, working on her pictures. She had decided to arrange them in a special binder, complete with captions, so they'd be all ready for the contest. She had to admit that they weren't really very good photographs. Maybe the next roll would be better.

By this time the living room curtains had been closed, but Connie could not forget the bottles on the window sill. She hadn't had a chance all day to look at them when no one else was around. She limped across the room and pulled aside the curtains.

Each bottle had a different shape and color. The first one was bright emerald green, decorated with a partridge-in-a-pear-tree whose tail swirled all the way around to the back. For the third day of Christmas, the bottle was shaped like a little blue cottage, and Connie smiled at the sight of the three French hens perched on its roof.

She moved on to the tall, slim bottle of milk glass. With a finger she traced the outline of the seven swans that swam across its shiny white surface. No wonder it was Aunt Laura's favorite. Taking a step backward, she studied the two rows of bottles: lemon yellow, deep purple, bright pink—all those beautiful colors! Why had Philip Hendrick especially mentioned the swan bottle? It wasn't transparent like the others were. Had he put something in it?

She took it from the window sill and lifted the white stopper that fitted neatly into its neck. Eagerly she peered inside. No, it was empty.

Slowly she began to put the stopper back on. She glanced at it and then took a closer look. Something white was coiled inside the hollow white dome. With a finger she nudged out a tightly rolled strip of paper. It fell into a long, dangling curl, and she held it up with growing excitement.

"Connie?" That was Mother, coming in from the kitchen.

"Yes?" She looped the paper strip around her finger, making a small white roll that slipped easily into her pocket.

"How about hamburgers for supper? I'm too tired to do much cooking tonight."

"Sounds great," Connie said. Suddenly everything was wonderful. "I'll help you."

All through supper, that roll of paper seemed to sizzle in Connie's pocket. The first chance she had, she limped up the stairs to her bedroom. Now she could really look at it.

The strip seemed to be made of ordinary white paper, and it was as long as her arm but only half an inch wide. Oddly enough, there were holes punched in it. The holes seemed to have been made by an ordinary hole punch, but they were spaced at irregular intervals all along the strip.

She sat down on the bed, curling and uncurling it around her finger, puzzling over it. Finally she decided that it must be a grille.

For one of their summer games, Dan had made up a letter with secret instructions in it that she couldn't figure out until she made use of an odd piece of paper. He had called it a 'grille.' It had holes cut into it that marked certain words as the hidden message.

She reached for the paragraph that she had copied out for Aunt Laura and positioned the strip carefully across the first line. The holes in the strip showed part of two words: *morning* and *the.*

She shook her head and moved the strip down to the next line of words. This time it picked out *sunrise.*

She stared at the words in dismay, then almost laughed aloud in relief. Of course. The grille was made to fit the original paragraph in the diary, not the copy she had written out. She'd just have to go and get the diary from the study.

She eased through the secret door, careful not to bump her ankle, and slid the panel closed behind her. When she reached the study, she switched on the light and stopped short. Something was wrong in here.

The chair had been knocked away from the desk, for one thing. And the set of diaries, usually so neat on their shelf, had spilled sideways. She took a quick, uneasy breath and limped closer to the desk. The next-to-last diary, the green one, was gone.

Chapter Fourteen
That Letter

It couldn't be.

Connie picked up the diaries one by one and checked their dates. The green one she had found behind the books was certainly missing.

Suddenly she was afraid. She backed away from the desk, banging her ankle painfully on something, and leaned against the door.

It was bad enough that she needed that diary in order to decode the message. But now someone else was looking for the shell too—she was sure of it—and he knew that the answer was in the green diary.

So he had come in here and stolen it.

She turned the doorknob and stumbled out into the hall. Dan, just going into his room, stopped and stared. "Hey, little sis, what's the matter? You look like you found a monster in there."

"Someone—" She had trouble getting the words out. "Someone—took the diary."

"What diary?" Dan followed her back into the room.

"Aunt Laura's husband had a whole bunch of diaries—there." She pointed to the shelf above the desk. "He mostly wrote about birds, but one of them told where he hid his golden cowrie—at least, Aunt Laura and I think it does. And now it's gone."

Slowly she added, "I think someone took it so he can find the shell before we do."

"When was the last time you saw this diary?" asked Dan calmly.

"Let's see—Friday night, I guess. Hey!" she exclaimed. "Remember when that guy tried to break in here last week? Maybe that's what he was after."

"Could be," Dan said. "But when could anyone have sneaked in here since Friday?"

"Saturday we were gone. Except for Aunt Laura and Mother."

Slowly Dan added, "And when Mother was outside, Mr. Stafford was here, visiting Aunt Laura. Of course, they were downstairs and might not have heard a burglar." He picked up a yellow-covered diary and frowned at it.

"Should we tell Aunt Laura?" asked Connie.

"Let's wait," Dan said quietly. "First of all, make sure it's really gone. Maybe it fell behind the desk or something. Then suppose we try figuring it out, instead of worrying her about it."

Connie resisted the impulse to tell him about the museum's offer to buy the shell. She couldn't really, because it was all tangled up with Aunt Laura's prayer secret. But she was glad that Dan knew about the shell now. This was getting more and more complicated.

After Dan left, she began to wonder if she really had put the diary back on the shelf as she'd meant to. Had she slipped it inside the desk? She switched on the desk lamp and rolled the desk top back, but she could see nothing green in any of the pigeonholes.

Next she opened the long, shallow drawer. It was full of letters that were bundled into small stacks. She could tell at a glance that there was no diary—unless it had been deliberately hidden here by someone.

It gave her an uncomfortable feeling to remember that when she first found the green diary, it was out of sight behind some books. Now she wondered if it had been hidden there on purpose. Absent-mindedly she sorted through the stacks of letters and then lifted the lid of a flat stationery box.

It held writing paper, just as she'd guessed. A letter in Philip Hendrick's handwriting lay open on top, and the inside address caught her eye.

It was addressed to the museum that had inquired about the golden cowrie. She glanced curiously at the date: March 12. That was just before he'd died, wasn't it? This could be important.

Without stopping to think about it, she skimmed through the letter. It stated that Philip Hendrick appreciated their interest in the golden cowrie but that the shell was not for sale. He would, however, agree to lend it to the museum for their exhibit.

Connie felt an icy thrust of disappointment. He didn't want to sell it. Why? She read through the letter again, more carefully. The only explanation he made was that he wanted to do this "for personal reasons," whatever that meant.

Slowly, jerkily, she closed the box and pushed it to the back of the drawer, wishing she had never found it. When Aunt Laura heard about this, she certainly wouldn't sell the golden cowrie. She wouldn't get the money she needed.

Connie stared at the row of diaries. There was no use in looking for the diary anymore, she thought, feeling defeated. It didn't matter. Let the shell stay hidden.

She stumbled back to her room and began getting ready for bed. If only she hadn't found that letter!

Suddenly she realized that she was the only one who knew about it. What if she just didn't say anything? Aunt Laura really did need the money.

As soon as she got into bed, plans for getting rid of the letter began to form in her mind. When something inside her protested, the plans would dissolve, only to reappear a minute later, like ghostly shapes drifting in and out of a fog.

After rearranging her pillow and pulling her sheet smooth for the fifth time, she told herself firmly, "No more thinking about that letter—not at all." At last she grew drowsy and drifted into an uneasy sleep.

When Connie awoke the next morning, she had a shadowy memory of nightmares, and for a moment she hoped that finding the letter had been just a bad dream. Then she began to remember details, and she sat up in bed with a sigh.

A heavy rat-a-tat on the door made her jump. Dan's voice called, "Mother says hurry up—and Aunt Laura's waiting to eat breakfast with you."

"Okay, I'm coming." A hurried look at the clock told her that she had overslept. Now she'd have to rush, and that was hard to do with a bad ankle.

While she ate breakfast with Aunt Laura, Connie had a chance to say something about the letter, but she pushed the idea away. Not yet. At least not until she'd thought about it a little more. And when her mother asked whether she wanted to go shopping, Connie agreed eagerly. She didn't really like to shop unless she had money to spend, but anything was better than staying here, where everything reminded her of the shell . . . and that letter.

Mother's shopping trip today consisted of short stops at several different stores, so Connie stayed in the car with her book. Later, on the way to the grocery store, Mother dropped her off at the town library so she could return her books.

They arrived home in time for a late lunch, and afterwards there was piano practice and math to be done. But Connie couldn't settle down to anything. It seemed like such a long time since she'd visited the marsh. Maybe she'd leave the math until tonight.

She limped out onto the back porch. "Connie, you be careful of that ankle," Mother called after her.

"I'll try," Connie said, and she let herself out the screen door. She found a hefty stick to lean on, and hobbled as far as the bluff that overlooked the marsh.

The sea was rippling gently with the outgoing tide, and it wore a pearly sheen under the soft grey sky. At the horizon, silvery light seeped in to outline the darker grey of a distant shore. Everything except the soaring gulls seemed to be wrapped in a quiet grey coverlet, waiting through the winter.

It's so peaceful, Connie thought. Not like me.

Restlessly she turned away, deciding to follow a path she hadn't noticed before. It slanted across the side of the bluff, and as she picked her way along it, she soon realized that it was taking her below Aunt Laura's house. Once past the bluff, it dipped down toward the marsh, becoming a muddy trail that meandered along the water's edge. Connie followed it mindlessly, not caring that her feet were beginning to get wet.

After a short distance, she came upon the place where she had met the man named Hank, and she eased herself down onto the rock. She was trying to decide whether to continue on the path, which sloped up into the woods, when she saw Coon. He was scampering towards her through the trees, closely followed by Ricky.

With a whistle for Coon, Ricky turned down the slope and halted in front of her. Coon leaped to his shoulder and they both peered down at her with bright, curious eyes. "Hi, whatcha doing?" Ricky asked, and then he chattered on, "I found a feather you might like. Have you got enough for your collection yet?"

"No," she admitted. "I'm going to have to find a lot more."

"Don't worry, I can find you plenty," he told her with a shy grin. "Want to see this one?"

"Sure."

"Okay, I'll bring it tomorrow. No, maybe I'll go get it." He started up the path and then hesitated, looking back at her. "Well, I guess you can come if you want. Just don't tell anybody. What happened to your foot?"

"Oh, I sprained my ankle," she said, pulling herself up. "What's this I'm not supposed to tell?"

"Where I keep my stuff." He led the way to where another fainter trail turned off, and then waited for her to catch up. "I've got a couple of hiding places. But this one is pretty close."

"You mean you keep your things outside?" Connie asked.

Ricky frowned, looking very grown-up. "My sister snoops," he said curtly. "And this is a special project."

He walked on in silence, finally stopping near an oak tree so huge that Connie thought it must be a hundred years old.

"Stay there," Ricky commanded. He darted around to the far side of the oak, reached into what must have been a hollow, and pulled out a round metal box. From where she stood, Connie could see that it was shiny red, the kind her mother kept cookies in at Christmas time.

Ricky turned his back on her, shielding the box from view, and took something from it. Then he put the box back in the hollow. He stood there for a minute longer, and Connie guessed that he was arranging some kind of camouflage over it.

"Here you are." He bounded over to her, holding out the feather. It was bright blue with several black bars and a white tip.

"Oh, how pretty!" Connie exclaimed. "What kind is it?"

"Probably came from a blue jay's tail," said Ricky, looking pleased with himself.

As they started off through the woods, Connie heard a noise that sounded like an animal growling in the distance. "What's that?" she asked, remembering the wild dog. "Maybe we'd better get out of here."

They stopped to listen. The growls alternated with whimpers and short, angry barks.

"He's not coming this way," Ricky observed. "Sounds like he's caught in a trap or something. Let's go see." He darted off through the trees, and Connie limped reluctantly after him.

Chapter Fifteen
"Be of Good Courage"

Before long the gloomy woods lightened, and Connie glimpsed a shabby-looking cabin in the clearing ahead of them. She caught up to Ricky, who was peering through a thicket of bushes.

"He's just tied up," Ricky said, sounding disappointed.

Beside the cabin, a ragged dog pulled and snapped at a chain anchored to an iron stake in the ground. The dog had scuffed a beaten path around the stake, and as they watched, it paced back and forth, growling.

Connie recognized its torn ear and she whispered, "That's the wild dog! Somebody's caught him and tied him up."

"I found out that Hank lives here," Ricky said slowly. "Guess he wanted a watchdog."

Connie smothered a giggle. "What in the world does he need a watchdog for, living in a shack like that?" Then she wished she hadn't said it. Ricky's house might not be much better.

To her surprise, Ricky chuckled. "Hank told me that he's got some valuable things in there. He collected them on a trip around the world." Connie couldn't understand

Ricky's grin until he added, "He needs protection from robbers like my raccoon, that's what."

Connie limped after him as he started back through the woods. "Did Coon take some of Hank's things?" she asked in amazement.

Ricky nodded. "A couple times. Just a few shells." He slowed his pace so she could walk beside him and gave her a sober, questioning look. "It's okay to do something that's a little bit bad so you can do something big that's good, isn't it?"

"What do you mean?" Connie asked cautiously.

"Well, I'm sure not giving those shells back."

Then he explained in a rush of words. "Hank doesn't need them, not as bad as I do—I'm keeping them to put on a box, to make it pretty for my mother. She's sick in the hospital, and she's been there a long time, and she needs something nice to cheer her up. So that makes it okay, doesn't it?"

Connie took a deep breath. "The only thing I know for sure," she said slowly, "is that when something's wrong, it's wrong. And even if you try to do good with it, God doesn't like it."

When Ricky didn't answer, she asked, "Can't you get something else to decorate your mother's box?"

Ricky shook his head decidedly. "Nope. If I was rich, I'd use pearls and jewels and gold—she's worth it. Never mind." By now they had reached the main path, and he turned away from her. "I've got to get home. See you later."

As he trotted off into the woods, she called after him, "Thanks for the feather." He gave her a quick wave and kept going.

What Ricky had said about jewels had given Connie an idea, though, and as soon as she got back to her bedroom, she took out her small jewelry box. Maybe she could find that string of pearls she had broken a couple of months ago. Half of the beads had rolled away when she'd dropped the necklace, but she had saved as many as she could.

One by one she picked out the pearls from the tangle in the bottom of her box. There weren't really enough of them for what Ricky wanted to do, but Mother might have something he could use too.

She limped down the hall to her mother's bedroom to ask.

"Yes," Mother said. "I've got one necklace that's all green and pink stones—it's too gaudy for me. You can have that."

It was just right, Connie thought, when Mother handed her the necklace. The stones were bright and shiny, and she knew Ricky would love them. Maybe now he'd be willing to return the shells that Coon had taken. Carefully she put the assortment of beads into a pillbox and slipped it into her jacket pocket so she'd have them the next time she went outside. You never knew when Ricky might show up.

After that she kept herself busy doing math problems and working on her school journal, and she almost managed to forget about the letter until it was bedtime.

When Dan poked his head into the room to ask about the stolen diary, she just told him that she hadn't found it yet and tried to look as if she had a lot of homework. While she changed her clothes, though, she began to wish she had someone who could tell her what to do.

I guess I should pray about it, she thought, but I'm too tired tonight. Resolutely she tried to think about other things as she lay in the darkness—about the swans, about Ricky, even about Dan. But it was a long time before she fell asleep.

All during breakfast the next morning, Connie waited uneasily for Aunt Laura to ask about the diary puzzle. But today her aunt seemed to be in a reminiscent mood. She told stories about the missionaries who had sent shells to her husband.

Then she added, "The golden cowrie was a special favorite of Philip's. We took a trip to the Fiji Islands so we could visit an old college friend. Our friend had a small church there, and he asked Philip to speak in the evening service. Several of the natives talked to us after the service, but one man in particular asked some searching questions about the Lord. His name was Mr. Kaho. After that, my husband invited him to come home with us for a meal. They met several times during the week, and one evening Mr. Kaho decided to receive Christ as his Saviour."

Aunt Laura's eyes sparkled at the memory. "At the end of our visit, Mr. Kaho presented my husband with the golden cowrie. It was so beautiful—we always said that it reminded us of heaven." She sighed. "I hate to think that something might have happened to it."

Connie felt a stab of guilt. How could she tell Aunt Laura that she'd given up on the shell?

Aunt Laura was gazing at her kindly. "You've been looking worried lately, Connie. I hope our prayer secret hasn't become a burden to you. I know it seems as if nothing is happening, but the Lord is going to answer, I'm sure of it. We've just got to wait until it's His time."

She handed Connie her Bible. "I think I've got that last verse of Psalm 27 memorized now. Check me on it, will you?"

Connie watched the verse while Aunt Laura said it:

Wait on the Lord: be of good courage, and he shall strengthen thine heart: wait, I say, on the Lord.

"You got it perfect!" she exclaimed, trying to sound more cheerful than she felt.

"Now if only I can live it," Aunt Laura said with a laugh. "Waiting has always been hard for me, so I keep reminding myself about the swans—waiting around in that photo blind isn't much fun, but it's worth it."

Connie nodded in agreement. Waiting was hard for her too. The words "be of good courage" rang in her memory. Even though she hadn't decided what to do about that letter, at least she could keep on trying to find the shell, couldn't she?

When she took Aunt Laura's tray back to the kitchen, Connie paused at the window to see what kind of day it was turning out to be. The pine trees, dripping wet, leaned somberly away from the wind that blew in from the sea.

"A cold, rainy day, isn't it?" Mother said, coming up behind her. "An indoors day. A clean-up-your-room day, Connie. Really, it looks like a rat's nest in there." She smiled, taking the edge off her words, but Connie knew she meant it.

While she worked on her room, she thought about how she could possibly find the shell without the diary. She had the grille, at least, and she had the paragraph too—although it wasn't much help the way she'd written it. If only she had hidden the diary instead of putting it back into the set!

By the time she finished her room and a few other chores, it was lunch time, and she couldn't help feeling that the whole morning had been wasted.

But one good thing had happened—she'd found the missing roll of film under her bed, so Stella could take it into town today with the rest. And now she was free for the afternoon. She glanced at the rain still drizzling down outside. First, she'd curl up on her bed and have a good read.

"Connie, you left your wastepaper basket in the hall," her mother reminded her. "You'd better empty it—and the kitchen garbage too."

That wouldn't take long. Connie dumped the garbage and the contents of her basket into a big, black plastic bag. The papers she had cleaned out of her room spilled into the black bag like a flurry of oversize snowflakes: Kleenex, crumpled math pages, lists of words she had experimented with when she was trying to decode Philip Hendrick's strange paragraph—

Wait! She snatched at one wrinkled sheet and smoothed it open with an exclamation of delight. The words on this page were just what she needed. She had copied them down when she'd been trying to arrange the beginning and ending words of each line into some kind of message. It hadn't solved anything, of course, but now she could use those words to figure out where each line in the original paragraph ended. Then the grille would work.

Quickly she tied up the plastic bag and carried it outside. She hurried back upstairs and grabbed for a pencil. Maybe she could rewrite the paragraph in its original form.

She borrowed another volume of the diary from the study and examined Philip Hendrick's writing carefully. Good thing he always made his entries in the same way. It seemed that every line he wrote was the same length, with every word precisely spaced.

Carefully she recopied the paragraph onto a fresh sheet of paper, trying to make her writing small and neat to match his. After doing a second copy, she was ready to use the grille.

She placed one end of the paper strip over the beginning of the first sentence. The single hole punched in the strip fell on the word *this*. But nothing seemed to fit the second line.

"I'm still doing something wrong," she muttered. "Is there another way to try it?"

She turned the strip of paper over and began with its other end. That was better. There was only one hole punched for this line, but it showed the word *hid*. And a faint crease in the paper matched the end of the line. She used that crease to help position the grille over the second line of words. The two holes in the strip revealed *golden* and *sea*. She hesitated over them, wondering what they meant, then decided to find the rest of the words before she tried to figure it out.

Using the grille to decode the next five lines, she scribbled down more words with rising excitement. Finally she had a sentence. *Hid golden sea second birdhouse past lookout.* It took only a second to realize that he was using *sea* to mean *c.* or "cowrie."

Now all I have to do is go down by the Lookout Tree to get the shell, she thought. . . . If it's still there. Her excitement began to fade. And if she found the shell, then what? She couldn't give it to Aunt Laura until she'd decided what to do about the letter.

With an odd mixture of reluctance and hope, Connie reached for her jacket. At least she could make sure the shell was still there.

Once outside the house, she found that the drizzling rain had stopped, although dark clouds still hung low. The shadows in the pine woods seemed deeper than ever, and as she hurried out of the trees, she heard a sound behind her—a twig snapping, perhaps? She turned quickly, straining her eyes into the gloom, but saw nothing. On her way across Deer Meadow, she wondered uneasily about that other person who wanted the shell.

At last she reached the Lookout Tree. Only a short distance farther was the second birdhouse.

Before she reached it, she stopped and looked back. The meadow lay silent and empty, winter-brown under the dull sky.

Curious now, she stepped closer to the birdhouse and peered into the small round hole at the front. It seemed to be filled with twigs. She examined the sides of the little grey box to see how it was made, and discovered a latch on the back.

She had to push hard on the rusted hook of the latch, but finally it lifted off and the whole back of the birdhouse swung open. There, among the twigs and grass and bits of fluff, she could see something white. Her fingers suddenly clumsy with eagerness, she worked it out from between the interlaced twigs of the nest. It was the right size and shape—she could feel that— and it was wrapped in a white handkerchief.

Chapter Sixteen
Found—or Lost?

Connie pulled off the handkerchief and knew immediately that she held a golden cowrie. Even in the dull grey dusk of the winter day, it seemed to have a golden orange glow. When she rolled it over, she saw that its glossy underside was trimmed in white. It felt wonderfully smooth in her hands, as if its sheen had come from endless polishings.

Her admiration turned into a sigh. Now, what to do with it? Coming to a hasty decision, she rewrapped the shell, thrust it back into the twigs, and closed up the birdhouse. It would have to stay here until she made up her mind. She trudged back across the field.

As she drew near the house, she decided to go on down to the photo blind, where Stella was probably working. Stella had been concerned about the prowler breaking into the study; she should be told that now something had actually been taken. Dan had talked about the stolen diary a couple of times too, but she didn't want to tell him about the letter she had found—it was all so complicated. But maybe Stella would have some ideas about how to find the thief.

When Connie reached the bluff, she caught sight of Dan and Ricky on the lower path to the marsh. It looked as if they had been talking, but as Connie watched, Ricky spun around and left Dan standing there, staring after him with an unhappy look on his face.

Then Dan turned and climbed the bluff, his head bent and his shoulders sagging. Connie met him halfway. He looked up at her and she saw the discouragement in his eyes.

"Tried to tell Ricky about the plan of salvation," he mumbled. "He treated me like I had the plague or something. I sure messed things up."

Connie wanted to ask him more about it, but he kept on walking, so she let him go. She remembered the beads in her pocket. Maybe she could still catch up with Ricky. She hurried along the muddy path, trying to move quickly in spite of her ankle.

She rounded a bend and glimpsed the familiar brown jacket. Ricky must have seen her, for he threw a glance over his shoulder, but he ducked off the path, disappearing into a thicket of prickly evergreens.

"Hey, Ricky," she called, almost slipping in the mud. "Wait, I've got something for you." When she reached the evergreens, she stood there and called again, "Come on—I don't bite—I just want to give you something."

He came back then. She heard a rustling in the evergreens and a moment later he stood next to her. He had an odd, closed look on his face, as though he were trying to shut her out. Dan couldn't have upset him that much, could he?

She held out the pill bottle. "Here, I got these for decorating your box." She opened it, letting the pearls and her mother's beads spill into her palm. "I think they're pretty, don't you?"

He only grunted in answer, but his eyes did not move from the shimmering beads as she rolled them back into the bottle and snapped on the top.

When he made no move to take it, she tucked the bottle into the pocket of his jacket, saying, "They're yours if you can use them." She turned to go. "I guess you're off somewhere in a hurry, so maybe I'll see you later."

"Okay." He scampered away, and she walked on to find Stella, feeling sorry for both Ricky and Dan.

That evening Connie sat down with her school project and tried to work on it as usual, but her thoughts wandered uneasily to the diary that had been stolen. Talking with Stella today had been a help, but it hadn't solved anything. They had discussed every detail they could think of in connection with the odd things that seemed to be happening to Aunt Laura.

First Aunt Laura had seen a face at her window, and then somebody had broken into her house during a storm. That was when she had been pushed down the stairs. Even if Aunt Mabel chose to scoff, Connie believed it.

Then a man had tried to get into Philip Hendrick's study. Later he must have tried again and succeeded, but all he had taken was the diary.

As she thought about it, Connie stroked the downy tip of the blue jay feather that Ricky had given her. She hadn't said anything to Stella about Aunt Laura's prayer secret or her own plan to find the golden cowrie, but she sure wished she could have.

She finished taping the feather into her notebook, still thinking about Aunt Laura. Her aunt kept saying that the Lord had a plan for the house and that He'd provide the money if He wanted the mission to have it. "Selling the golden cowrie has got to be the best way to do it," Connie told herself firmly as she closed her notebook and stood up. But the letter! It really did sound as though Philip Hendrick hadn't wanted to sell that particular shell, and now that she knew it had been a special gift, she understood why.

"Surely he wouldn't mind," Connie argued with herself, "—not if he knew how badly his wife needs the money."

Restlessly she walked out onto the balcony. She pulled the white chair close to the railing and leaned her head against a post to watch the dark, tranquil woods. There were no stars. The night was so still that she thought she could hear the gentle murmur of the tide, far down in the marsh.

Aunt Laura will get that money if I just keep quiet about Philip Hendrick's letter to the museum, she thought. That isn't so terrible, is it?

Immediately she remembered the question that Ricky had asked her yesterday. Wasn't she asking the same thing? She shifted uncomfortably at the thought of her answer: *"When something's wrong, it's wrong."*

For another long moment she stared into the darkness, struggling with the confusion of feelings inside her, and then she slowly got to her feet. She stepped back into her bedroom and flopped onto the bed. "I'm sorry, Lord," she whispered. "I thought I had it all figured out—how You were going to answer Aunt Laura's prayer. I guess I just don't know what Your plan is.

Maybe Your answer is 'No.' " She took a deep breath. "But what should I do now?"

She rolled over and fluffed up her pillow and thought about it. At least she knew one thing she had to do. Tomorrow morning, first thing, she would go back and get the shell.

When Connie awoke, it was much earlier in the morning than usual. She sat up, feeling uneasy. In her dreams she had spent all night looking for the shell— looking and looking and never finding it. She fumbled through her clothes for something warm to wear and then sleepily pulled on her jacket.

As soon as she stepped outside, the cold, salty wind whipped into her face, snapping her wide awake. The whole world was misted and grey in the shadowy light of dawn. Slowly she crossed the back lawn, and the frozen grass crunched startlingly loud under her feet.

Once she had passed through the gloom under the pine trees and Deer Meadow was in sight, she expected her uneasiness to lift. But now she felt a sudden urgency to get there: to see the shell, to handle it, to know that it was safe. *Hurry-hurry* something inside her muttered in time to her quick footsteps. *Hurry-hurry-what-if-what-if—*

She broke into a hobbling run and flung herself awkwardly across the frosty meadow, not stopping until she had reached the birdhouses. The second one. Quickly she unlatched the hook and swung open the small wooden door.

There was no white-wrapped object inside. Only darkness.

She riffled frantically through the twigs, even though she knew that if the shell were there, it would be easy to see. Perhaps in her hurry she had come to the wrong birdhouse? She glanced up at the Lookout Tree, looming grey in the mist, and counted again. No, this was the one. Unwilling to give up, she ran to the birdhouses on either side, pried open each rusty latch, and peered in. One was completely empty and the other was half-filled with dead grass. The shell was gone.

There was nothing to do but go back. *Gone.* The word echoed hollowly in her mind as she stumbled across the rough grass. *Gone,* and it was her fault, too. If she had taken it yesterday when she'd had the chance, Aunt Laura would have it right now. If only she hadn't been so stubborn about that letter!

Gone. But where? Had someone figured out the puzzle in the diary? Or had someone followed her yesterday?

Nervously she glanced over her shoulder at the broad meadow behind her, brightening now with sunrise. The sun itself was still veiled by clouds and appeared only as a blurred spot of gold in the leaden sky. But it gave enough light so that she didn't mind walking back under the pines. On the way, someone in a grey jacket passed her—the man Hank. He seemed to be in a hurry and gave her only a nod.

Her thoughts were still circling anxiously around the problem of the shell. Yesterday, anyone could have hidden in those woods near the birdhouses—could have seen her take it out—could have come back last night and stolen it.

In a panic of despair, she began to run, arriving breathless at the porch of Aunt Laura's house. She stood there for a minute, panting, wondering what to do next.

Stella. She'd tell Stella about it and Stella would help.

Immediately Connie felt better. She entered the house, hoping no one would ask where she'd been, and began her job of helping with breakfast.

"Well, you have rosy cheeks," her mother said, looking up from the eggs she was scrambling. "Been out for a walk? Isn't the sun beautiful behind the clouds like that?"

"Yes," mumbled Connie, and busied herself with Aunt Laura's tray. She was afraid to say anything, afraid she'd burst into tears and have to tell the whole story. As soon as breakfast was over, she'd find Stella.

She carried Aunt Laura's tray into the bedroom, trying to think of something to talk about—anything but the shell. To her relief, Aunt Laura seemed unusually thoughtful this morning and ate her meal without saying much at all.

Just before they prayed together, Aunt Laura said quietly, "Did your mother tell you about Stella?"

"No, what?" asked Connie.

"She had to leave. Her mother became very ill and they called for her late last night."

Connie gripped her cup in hands that had suddenly become cold. "She's gone?" she whispered.

"Yes," said Aunt Laura with a sigh. "I knew you'd miss her. I will too." She picked up an envelope from her bedside table and took a letter out of it. "Did you tell her about our prayer secret?"

"No, I didn't." Connie shook her head emphatically.

Aunt Laura unfolded the letter and showed Connie the check inside. "She left some money—she said it was to pay for the time she spent here, although I told her not to."

"Oh, good!" exclaimed Connie. "How much? I mean—is it enough to pay off the debt?"

"It's not quite enough," Aunt Laura said, "but I'm taking it as an encouraging sign from the Lord that He'll send the rest of it in His own time." She smiled and picked up a second envelope, handing it to Connie. "There's a letter for you, too."

"Thank you." Connie slipped the envelope into her pocket. She would open it later when she could be alone. Aunt Laura must have understood how she felt, for her prayer was brief, but it was full of praise. Connie added a silent plea for help. She still had to get that shell back, and now Stella was gone.

As soon as the breakfast things had been cleared away, Connie limped upstairs to read Stella's letter. It was warm and friendly, just the kind of letter Stella would write. After explaining that her mother was sick, Stella had said that she'd come back in a few days— as soon as she could—because she was still concerned about Aunt Laura.

Connie looked away from the letter in dismay. Stella wouldn't get back in time. Not before Aunt Mabel came on Friday. Not before they had to leave.

Maybe she could phone her—I've got to talk to Stella, she thought desperately. So she can tell me—

What would Stella say?

Connie's racing mind quieted, remembering. She knew what Stella would say. Stella had already told her *"don't go getting impatient with God's plan—He'll show you when He's good and ready."*

But I've asked Him to show me what to do about the shell, and now this has happened, Connie thought. And everything keeps getting worse.

She wandered to the window, and her gaze turned automatically to the marsh. She pictured the swans in their pond—paddling around and feeding peacefully, so beautiful that they hardly seemed real. What had Aunt Laura said about them? ". . . worth waiting for."

And then there was Aunt Laura's verse about waiting. *"Wait on the Lord: be of good courage, and he shall strengthen thine heart. . . ."* It seemed that all she could do about the shell was wait. Was that what He wanted? Okay.

Connie went back to Stella's letter. It closed by asking if Connie would mind picking up her film when she went into town to get hers.

Yes, she could do that, at least. It would be a relief to do something—anything. And Connie was curious about how her own pictures had turned out. There would be two rolls this time—the one she'd found under the bed and one with the pictures she'd taken of the swans. She hurried downstairs to find out when Mother could take her into town.

"I was just thinking about another shopping trip," her mother said in answer to the question. "With Aunt Mabel coming on Friday and your father on Saturday, we'll need some more groceries." She explained to Aunt Laura, "Stella asked Connie to pick up the film she's had developed."

"That's nice," Aunt Laura said. "Stella mentioned that we might want to look at her pictures. She thinks she got some fairly good close-ups of a pair of mute swans."

As soon as they got back from town, Connie took the picture packets into Aunt Laura's bedroom.

"I'm coming into the living room, so you don't all have to crowd in here with me," Aunt Laura announced with a smile.

"Are you sure you feel up to it?" asked Mother anxiously.

"Yes, indeed." Aunt Laura's dimples deepened in her plump cheeks. "I'm much better and I'm going to start moving around." She sat up very straight in bed and began pulling on a pink robe. "Connie, if you'll look in the top drawer of the bureau by the window, you'll find one of those little slide viewers. We'll start with that."

Chapter Seventeen
The Mysterious Fisherman

While Mother helped Aunt Laura walk to the living room sofa, Connie found the slide viewer. Aunt Laura dropped a slide into the slit in the viewer, and the small square screen lit up to illuminate the picture.

They passed the slide viewer back and forth, admiring the slides one by one. The pictures that Stella had taken from the airplane showed a wide panorama of water and marsh and coastline. Connie compared them with her glossy prints. Most of hers were a little blurred, but she still had one or two that she could be proud of. She showed Aunt Laura her shot of the dog and the snow goose.

"Yes, that's a good one," agreed Aunt Laura. "I wonder what ever happened to that dog. It just seemed to disappear."

"We saw it the other day," Connie told her. "It was tied up outside a cabin in the woods. A man lives there—he's a college student or something—and he's studying marsh grass. His name is Hank. Have you met him?"

"No, although I think I know which cabin you mean. It's been empty for a while—he must be renting it. Strange that he would want a dog like that." She shrugged. "Well, let's look at the other box of slides. I'd like to see the ones that Stella took of the swans."

Connie opened the next package and dropped a slide into the viewer. "Here are your swans," she said, passing it to Aunt Laura.

"Yes, there they are, the lovely things," Aunt Laura said happily. Mother leaned over to look at it too.

Connie scanned the next few slides, holding them up to the light. "Here are some close-ups."

One by one, Aunt Laura looked at them. "Oh, what beautiful birds! Stella must have used her telephoto lens for these shots. Look at this one, Connie, she's caught someone—there's a man in the background."

As Connie leaned over to take a look, Aunt Laura exclaimed, "I know that man! Now, where have I seen him before?"

Connie recognized him right away. "That's Hank, the student I was telling you about."

Aunt Laura shook her head, murmuring, "No, I don't think that's his name. Where do I know him from? That hair—his face is different—maybe . . ."

She frowned at the slide, studying it. "Connie, there's a slide projector in my husband's study on the bottom shelf near the desk. Could you get it for me? It would be nice to see all of these enlarged, anyway."

"Sure." Connie hurried upstairs, almost running into Dan, who was on his way down.

"Where are you hobbling to so fast?" he said with a grin.

"I'm getting the slide projector for Aunt Laura," she said over her shoulder as she passed him. "We're looking at Stella's slides."

Dan turned and followed her. "I'd like to see those too," he said, "I'll help you with that." He carried the projector downstairs and set it up for them.

"Stella took some close-ups of the swans, and there's one with a man in it," Connie explained to him. "Aunt Laura's trying to figure out who he is."

Dan focused the projector on the living room wall, and Aunt Laura handed him the slide.

In the center of the picture was the pair of swans, sleek and white, with the sun gleaming on their feathers. At the edge of the pond, partly hidden by tall grass, stood a man. He seemed to be watching the swans.

"Yes, I'm sure I used to know him, only his hair is longer now, and it looks different with that hat on," Aunt Laura said firmly. She sat in silence for a few minutes. Connie stared at the tanned face on the screen and tried to remember everything that Ricky had told her about Hank.

Aunt Laura let out a sigh. "Yes, it's Tatum," she said slowly. "Henry Tatum. Maybe his nickname is Hank, but we always called him Tatum." Connie felt a chilly prickle down the back of her neck. She recognized that name. Aunt Laura was saying, "Funny thing, I never thought I'd see him again. He's shaved off his mustache, too."

Connie kept silent with an effort. Dan always said she went off half-cocked about things. She'd make sure about that name before she said anything.

They looked at the slides that were left, and while Aunt Laura, Mother, and Dan were discussing the way Stella had used a certain lens in one of her shots, Connie took a quick look at the rest of her own pictures.

They're much better this time—I even have a pretty good one of the swans, she thought. She picked up the picture she had taken of the fisherman by the marsh pond. Now, of course, she knew that it was Hank: she could tell by his blue knitted cap. She handed the picture to Aunt Laura. "Do you think this is the same man as the one in Stella's picture?"

"Yes," said Aunt Laura after a moment. "I can't see his face very clearly, but I'd recognize that nose anywhere. See his profile?" She pointed it out to Connie while Dan, looking on, nodded in agreement. Connie put the picture back on the pile. She'd look at it again, when she was by herself.

Dan picked it up and studied it. "Hey, this isn't a bad shot—the way you've got him silhouetted against the water. The colors are interesting, too. What else have you got here?"

He sorted through her pictures while she watched uneasily. "I like this one—it looks like a kid I knew last year." With a grin, he showed them her photo of a Canada goose strutting along the dike. "You ought to enter some of these in the photo contest at school."

"I was hoping they'd be good enough," Connie told him, encouraged by his praise.

That evening, while she was arranging her photographs in their album, she took another careful look at them, especially the one of the fisherman.

She was glad that Dan had liked it. But somehow she felt differently about the photo contest now. She still wanted to win, but she wasn't going to depend on that to decide her whole future. In fact, she wasn't all that certain anymore that she would make a very good professional photographer.

Talking to Stella had made her feel better about whatever God had planned for her, though. She smiled to herself, remembering Stella's imitation of her grandma's Southern drawl. "I reckon . . . He'll show you when He's good and ready. . . ."

Her gaze fell on the fisherman's face, half-turned away in the picture. Aunt Laura had called him *Tatum*.

That reminded her. Connie jumped up. She'd read something about a man named Tatum in one of Philip Hendrick's diaries. What had he said? She'd better find out.

It took only a minute to get into the study, and she soon had the yellow diary in her hand. Quickly she skimmed through the pages of bird sightings. It was somewhere near the end of this one—there. Philip Hendrick had found Tatum snooping in the shell room, and because of it, he'd started to think about hiding the golden cowrie.

Connie put the little book back on the shelf, frowning thoughtfully. Too bad she didn't have the last volume, because it had referred to Tatum again. Now that she thought about it, she was sure Philip Hendrick had said he'd fired him because the man was stealing his shells.

Slowly she returned to her room. Now it was all beginning to fit together. This Tatum person was still hanging around, pretending to be a student so he could steal the golden cowrie.

She picked up the photo that she had labeled "Lonely Fisherman." She'd taken it because she thought the colors were pretty: the fisherman in his blue jacket and cap, with the blue water and the gleaming marsh behind him. Now he looked almost sinister as he sat there pretending to be a fisherman—and all the time planning how he could steal—

Suddenly Connie remembered the torn piece of fabric she had found after the prowler had tried to break into the study. She grabbed for her jacket and pulled the scrap out of a pocket. Yes, it looked like the same shade of blue.

But the jacket that Tatum wore around here was grey. If it weren't for the picture, she'd never have connected him with a blue jacket.

When had she taken that picture, anyway? She hunted up the little red notebook that she used for keeping track of her pictures. The date showed that she had taken it the first Monday she was here. And the break-in was Monday night. He could have noticed that the jacket was ripped and decided not to wear it again.

Connie began putting her things away. It was scary to think that all this time Hank must have been watching the house, watching her, waiting for a chance to steal the shell. And now he had it. She stopped, holding a book in midair. Or did he? Hank hadn't looked very happy when she'd met him on the path today. Besides, wouldn't he have disappeared when he got what he wanted? But if he didn't have the shell, where was it?

The next morning, Connie was kept so busy that she hardly had time to think about the shell. There were two coconut cream pies to make, besides other things for the special meal Mother was planning to have tomorrow. And Mother was on another house-cleaning spree. At first Connie thought it odd, since they'd just cleaned last week, but then she decided that it must be because of Aunt Mabel's visit.

Aunt Mabel was a fanatic when it came to anything that she called 'filth.' She could find 'filth' in places that looked just fine to Connie, and then she would frown and mutter about mothers who went off gallivanting instead of properly caring for their families. It always made Connie bristle when Aunt Mabel referred to Mother's painting that way, but Mother never would talk back to her.

While she vacuumed the living room, Connie had a chance at last to puzzle over the shell. It didn't do any good, though. She just couldn't come up with any kind of satisfactory answer.

Finally she decided that she'd better tell someone how suspicious she was about Hank. Not Aunt Laura or Mother. They had enough on their minds with Aunt Mabel coming tomorrow. Dan knew part of it; should she tell him the rest?

Connie sighed to herself and unplugged the vacuum. She'd wanted to solve this on her own, and here she was running to Dan with it. That wasn't very grown-up.

She dragged the vacuum down the hall, slid it into the closet, and shut the door with a decisive click. Never mind what Dan thought of her. The important thing right now was Aunt Laura's shell.

Right after lunch, Connie followed Dan up to his room and told him the whole story of the missing shell. He listened intently and then asked what she thought was going on.

"I think it's this Tatum," said Connie. "If he used to work here, he'd know about the shell and how valuable it is. Maybe he even knew that the museum wanted to buy it." She could just picture him poking through Philip Hendrick's desk.

"Go on," said Dan. "Anything else?"

"Well, there's the man who tried to break into the study. Remember I already told you about the blue jacket? I'm sure it had to be someone like Tatum, because he used the secret door. A stranger wouldn't have known about that."

"What secret door?" Dan ran a hand through his blond hair, looking puzzled.

"I'll show you." Connie led him into her bedroom and took him through to the shell room, showing him how the door worked. From his grin, she could tell that Dan was impressed.

"I thought that was some wild thing you dreamed when you talked about seeing the man in your bedroom," he told her.

"I wondered myself if I had dreamed it," Connie admitted. "But then I discovered the door."

Dan gazed silently at the drawers of shells all around them, and Connie tried to wait patiently while he was thinking.

"What about Ricky?" he said at last. "Maybe he knows something about this guy that will help us."

"He's never said much about Hank," Connie answered. "But let's ask him. He's usually around here somewhere in the afternoons."

Dan followed her out of the study. "I can't go with you right away. I've got a bunch of windows to finish washing for Mother."

Connie groaned. "Well, I hope Aunt Mabel is properly impressed. We've sure worked hard enough to get this place cleaned up. How long will it take you?"

"About an hour, I guess." Dan started downstairs with Connie behind him.

"Okay, maybe I'll go talk to Ricky, and by the time I get back you'll be done."

"Good," Dan said. "Then we can figure out what to do next."

Connie stopped off at the kitchen to get an apple and a couple of cookies. She was surprised to find herself humming as she left the house. *We* Dan had said. They were working together now, and that made her feel good.

Chapter Eighteen
Oh, Coon!

Connie stood for a moment on the back porch, studying the cloudy sky and wondering where to look for Ricky. She turned left, toward Deer Meadow. Ricky always seemed to come from this direction, and Hank's cabin was this way too.

As she walked along, she nibbled on a cookie and thought about Ricky. He'd been the one who had introduced her to Hank. Did he know what kind of a person Hank really was?

She hesitated at the fork in the trail, and as she stood there, she heard footsteps pounding toward her. It was Ricky. He burst out of the woods, cradling something in his arms. She ran to meet him, and he held out an armful of dark fur.

"Look at Coon," he sobbed. "Look what Hank did to Coon."

"What's the matter with him?" Connie helped Ricky to lay the unconscious coon on a smooth place beside the path.

She ran her fingers gently over the small, limp body. "I can feel his heart beating," she said. "He's not bleeding anywhere, is he? What happened?" She stroked the coon, wondering what to do for it.

Ricky dashed the tears from his eyes with an angry swipe of his sleeve. He hunched down close to Coon and muttered, "That Hank, he threw him out. He slammed Coon onto the ground and then left him there for the dog to kill."

"How come?"

"Oh, Coon must have gotten into his shells again, and Hank caught him at it." Ricky lifted one of Coon's paws and curved the long claws around his finger. "I got in there fast and picked him up, and he was still holding onto a shell—he sure likes the pretty ones."

"Look, he's moving," whispered Connie. The young coon stirred and groaned, sounding so much like a human baby that Connie wanted to hug him. But she remembered a warning her father had given her about injured animals.

"Don't get too close," she told Ricky, whose face was next to the coon's. "If something's hurting him, he might bite you." Looking reluctant, Ricky sat back on his heels and watched.

The small coon stirred again and opened his eyes. For a minute he looked dazed; then he sat up and hobbled over to Ricky, whimpering softly. Ricky gathered him into his arms and murmured soothingly to him. The coon settled down with a sigh under Ricky's gentle stroking.

Ricky gave Connie a grateful glance. "Good thing I ran into you. I sure didn't know what to do."

Connie started to reply but he went on hurriedly, "I've got to tell you something I did—something really bad. It's about that orange shell."

He avoided her eyes, fastening his gaze on the coon. "See, a while ago, that man, Hank, told me he wanted to write something for a magazine about your aunt. He said he'd pay me if I asked you questions and found out stuff about her husband's shell collection."

Connie exclaimed in surprise, and Ricky went on in a rush of words. "So then after a while he told me to watch you and see where you went, and one day I saw you find that orange shell in the birdhouse, and I told him about it. He said he wouldn't pay me nothing unless I got it for him." Ricky threw her a worried glance and looked away again.

"So I went back later on and took it." He ducked his head away as if he expected her to hit him and added quickly, "But I didn't have time to give it to him that night. I hid it in a special place by my house, and then I got to thinking about it and I knew it was wrong. And all the time I was feeling bad about the shells of his that I kept—remember I told you?"

Connie nodded hurriedly.

"So I took those back to him today, and that's when Coon got into his stuff again. And by then I wished I hadn't taken that orange shell." He sighed.

"It was a bad thing I did," he went on mournfully. "And I've done other bad stuff too. Your brother said that God punishes people when they do wrong things. But you said God loves people."

"He does!" exclaimed Connie. "Both of those things are true—the Bible tells all about it, how God sent His Son Jesus to take the punishment for the wrong things and—"

"Yeah," Ricky interrupted. "Your brother said something about that too. He kept saying some verses from the Bible. I guess I need to talk to him again. But I felt so awful that day because it was right after I'd watched you with the shell at the birdhouse." He glanced up at her from under his tangled mop of hair. "Do you think Dan's mad 'cause I wouldn't listen?"

"No," Connie said. "He'd talk to you anytime."

Ricky changed the subject abruptly. "I guess you've been worried about that orange shell, haven't you?"

"Yes." Connie felt the excitement churning inside her, and she tried to keep her voice calm. "That shell is really important to Aunt Laura."

The coon, still in Ricky's arms, yawned widely and closed its eyes. Ricky sat there watching it, and Connie began to wonder if he'd forgotten about the shell.

"Are you sure the shell is safe?" she asked at last. "Can't you go get it?"

"Yeah, I guess so. I didn't want to wake up Coon." Ricky got to his feet, still cradling the raccoon. "Do you think he'll be all right?"

"I hope so. Maybe he just got knocked out," Connie said. "I'll go with you to get the shell," she offered, half-afraid that he wouldn't come back with it.

"Okay—it's over by my house."

He sounded relieved, and as Connie followed him down the trail, she wondered if he was worrying about running into Hank Tatum. He'd really be scared if he knew that the man was a thief. After the shell was safely back in Aunt Laura's hands, she'd tell Ricky all about Hank Tatum. Then maybe they could get the man put in prison.

She glanced at the clouds that seemed to be hanging just above the treetops, and she walked faster, hoping that Ricky's house was near. She would have to come back all this way by herself after she got the shell, and it was getting late. The path they followed now was unfamiliar, and she watched its turns carefully so she could find her way back.

The woods and the path ended abruptly at a road that had lost its pavement in a jumble of potholes. From where she stood, Connie could see a wide stretch of marsh, but the horizon was hidden by grey haze, and long, curling drifts of fog reached toward the shore. A dozen small houses built on pilings stood in a careless row beside the road, which ran straight out into the marsh and then disappeared, as if it had drowned.

"Stay here," Ricky said. "I'll put Coon in his house and then go get it. Be right back." Connie nodded, and she watched him run down the road to a faded blue house that huddled under a clump of pines.

He took the coon into a tool shed beside the house, pulling the door shut. Then he ran around behind the house, and Connie saw that he was heading for an ancient dock that leaned out across the tide pools and marsh grass. He ducked between two of the black pilings and reappeared a minute later with a satisfied look on his face.

He trotted back to the road, and Connie started forward to meet him, but as Ricky passed under the pine trees, a man stepped from the shadows and put a hand on his shoulder.

It was Hank Tatum. Connie couldn't make out his words, but she could hear his voice, and it was low and threatening. She guessed that he was asking about the shell. Ricky looked up at him and shook his head.

To Connie's amazement, Tatum picked up the boy and hustled him into a small car parked beneath the trees. The car leaped forward, sped around a bend in the road, and was out of sight.

Connie stared after it. Ricky hadn't even had time to yell. She threw an anguished glance at the silent houses. There'd be no help here. She had to get back to Aunt Laura's house to phone the police. She turned into the woods and began to run.

As she ran, she tried to think. Where would Tatum be taking Ricky? To his cabin? That was it. She'd check there on her way. She slowed her headlong pace so she wouldn't miss the narrow path that branched off towards the cabin.

It was getting harder to see: the fog must be moving in fast. It filled the woods with a silvery half-light that blurred everything into a bewildering haze. But she found the turnoff and hurried down it.

Ricky's giant oak tree loomed suddenly beside the path, its topmost branches wreathed in misty grey. Now she knew that she was getting close, and she picked her way quietly to the sheltered spot from which they had watched the dog.

The dog was still there, a furry shadow pacing aimlessly through drifting grey fog. But the small cabin looked deserted. Connie scanned its blank windows with growing dismay. Tatum would have been here by now.

She turned away hastily, regretting the time she had lost. He must have gone somewhere else. But where? It had to be someplace nearby, since Tatum probably didn't realize that Ricky had the shell with him, and he'd be in a hurry to come back to get it.

And Tatum would pick an isolated place, so that people wouldn't see. . . . Connie choked at the thought of what he might be doing to Ricky. Suddenly she

remembered the photo blind—that little wooden hut, almost invisible, that sat on the edge of nowhere. Hadn't Stella said it'd be a good place for smugglers?

She reached the main path and broke into a fast trot. A warning twinge of pain licked at her ankle, but she ignored it and tried to make some kind of plan. First she'd stop at the house and get Dan. He'd be wondering what had happened to her by now. And someone had better phone the police.

Deer Meadow went past in a haze. Then she was into the pine woods, and she felt as if she were rushing through a narrow tunnel with soft grey walls. At the far end, the fog was thicker than ever. It pressed coldly against her face, slowing her down and wrapping her with chilly despair. How am I ever going to find Ricky in all of this? she thought. What if he isn't at the photo blind?

As she neared the house, she strained her eyes through the shifting grey to look for Dan. Just as she'd hoped, he was waiting for her outside, and he'd brought a flashlight. He waved it at her with a worried expression on his face.

"Oh," she panted, "I'm so glad you're here. Hank Tatum got Ricky, because Ricky's got the shell. I think he took him out to the photo blind." She started toward the marsh. "Tell Mother to phone the police, and maybe Mr. Stafford too."

Dan stared at her for an instant, nodded, and then turned back to the house in his deliberate way. She couldn't stand to watch him move so slowly. "Hurry!" she cried. "Don't explain everything. I'm going on down to the photo blind."

At the bluff, she had to stop again to catch her breath.

The woods behind her lay hushed and dim. The marsh below was smothered in soft billows of fog, silent except for the whispering murmur of the tide. She wanted to linger in the blurred twilight, to let it calm the fearful pounding of her heart. But there was no time. Desperately she snatched at the memory of Aunt Laura's verse and claimed it for her own. *"Wait on the Lord: be of good courage, and he shall strengthen thine heart."*

The verse steadied her mind and spurred her to action. She began groping her way over the edge of the bluff, and Dan caught up with her before she was halfway down. Once they reached level ground, Connie wanted to run, to race to the photo blind at top speed, but here the fog was at its thickest. With every step they took, it gave way ahead and then closed behind, hemming them in, slowing them to a walk.

And the fog did strange things to the familiar landscape: small junipers turned into dark, fuzzy statues; the pile of wet boulders became a gleaming rampart wreathed in mist; even the ponds were changed into seething cauldrons of grey.

The going was easier once they found the path through the holly trees. The fog seemed thinner here, and the carpet of pine needles deadened the sound of their footsteps. Dan must have done as much exploring as Connie had, for he seemed to know his way in spite of the fog.

It occurred to her that they hadn't seen a car parked anywhere. Going by the road was a much longer way around, but he'd surely have been here by now. What if Tatum hadn't brought Ricky to the photo blind, after all? They would never, never find him. She resisted the thought. As they hurried through the trees, she concentrated on asking the Lord to show them what to do.

"Look," Dan whispered, "someone's in there." The blurred outline of the hut loomed ahead. Through one of the openings, Connie could see a flicker of light—perhaps from a flashlight. Dan crept silently around to the back side of the hut, and she followed.

From inside came a man's harsh whisper and the sounds of a struggle. Connie heard a whimper. That must be Ricky, she thought painfully. What was Tatum doing to him?

Ricky said something, ending with a low sob, and Connie winced. Then Tatum must have forgotten to whisper, for his voice carried clearly. "So you had it on you all the time, you crummy kid—" His voice subsided to a mutter.

Connie hunched close to the ground as footsteps thudded out of the hut. She started to jump up, to rush inside, but Dan touched her arm. "Wait," he whispered.

The seconds ticked by until at last, through the muffled stillness of the fog, they heard the faint growl of a departing car. Tatum must have hidden his car in the woods somewhere, she thought.

"Okay, let's go," Dan said.

Chapter Nineteen
Trailing Tatum

Connie rushed into the darkness of the hut and found Ricky squirming on the ground. He was tied and gagged. "Oh, are you all right?" she whispered. "Quick, Dan, where's your light?" She pulled the cloth off Ricky's mouth while Dan worked on the ropes.

"He found the shell," Ricky moaned. "He took it off me before I could hide it."

"Never mind, he won't get away," Connie said with more assurance than she felt.

They helped Ricky to his feet, and after a minute he was able to limp out the door. Slowly they started down the path. "Are you okay?" Connie asked him again.

"Yeah," he said. "Just a little stiff. It's getting better."

When they reached the gravel road, Ricky said, "I know a short cut back to your aunt's house."

"Let's take it," said Dan.

Connie couldn't understand how Ricky could tell where he was going, for they seemed to be moving in a world of rolling grey cloud. But he followed a faint trail of some kind, and before long they had reached the edge of the woods, just below Aunt Laura's house.

Ricky, still in the lead, stopped short. "Someone's coming," he whispered hoarsely. "Over there."

Connie peered through the fog. It was a man wearing a blue cap. What was Tatum doing here?

Rapidly he crossed the back lawn and entered the woods on the other side. "He's taking the path to the bluff," Ricky whispered. "Let's go this way."

He guided them down to the path that skirted the marsh, and Connie remembered that it was a more direct route to the bluff. But it was wetter. She could feel the mud squishing under her sneakers.

They drew near to the underside of the bluff. Connie saw that someone short and plump was climbing slowly upward, grunting as he went.

"Oh, that's Mr. Stafford," she whispered to Dan, glad for once to see the man. "He'll—" She froze as Tatum's voice floated down from the top of the bluff.

"Well, it's about time. You were supposed to be waiting here, remember? So I wouldn't have to stand around, like I'm doing right now."

"It took you long enough," Mr. Stafford complained, still puffing from the climb. "I couldn't just hang around—it'd look suspicious. Had to keep moving."

Dan took Connie's arm and eased her back into a clump of junipers. Ricky huddled beside them.

"Well, did you get it?" Mr. Stafford's deep voice was impatient.

"Sure did. But what about the kid? He's onto me now," muttered Tatum.

"That's your problem. If you'd gotten the diary the first time, like I told you, I'd be sitting in Arizona right now. But no, you had to go and mess things up—push the old lady down the stairs—"

"You know I didn't push her!" Tatum burst out. "It was an accident. I ran past her and she just fell—"

"Uh-huh. Who's going to believe that story?" Mr. Stafford's chuckle held a threat. "So you'd better hand over that shell and start running."

"Where's my money?"

"First the shell. Ah, yes . . ." Mr. Stafford let out a long wheezing breath, and Connie knew he was gloating over the beautiful golden cowrie. She tensed, and Dan clutched at her in warning.

"C'mon, the money," insisted Tatum.

"Okay, now get out of here."

The bushes rustled as Tatum left. Dan leaned over to Connie. "We can't let him get away," he whispered. "Ricky and I will try and trip him—up near the house. See if you can get Mr. Stafford up to the house too. The police ought to be here any minute."

"But how?" Connie gasped in dismay.

"He likes you—you can do it, sis." Dan disappeared into the swirling fog, leaving her to stare after him.

She could hear Mr. Stafford's heavy footsteps cross the bluff. He was starting toward the path to his house. She had to hurry if she was going to do anything at all.

She darted to the bottom of the bluff and began stumbling up the slope. "Mr. Stafford? Mr. Stafford!" Her voice seemed to melt into grey nothingness.

Where *was* he? She flung herself up the bank in desperate haste and she slipped, falling awkwardly across a clump of smooth, wet marsh grass.

"Oh!" Without meaning to, she cried aloud. A fiery stab of pain licked across her ankle.

"Who's there?"

Mr. Stafford's voice made her jump. She hadn't realized that he was still so close.

"It's me, Connie." Her voice came out as a croak of despair. And then she knew how she was going to get him to the house.

She lay where she had fallen and groaned loudly. Mr. Stafford's ponderous bulk appeared, like a huge dark ship in the sea of grey. "What's the matter?" He didn't sound the least bit friendly.

Connie pulled herself to her knees and groaned once more. The pain was real enough. "I—I fell and hurt my ankle again." She looked up at him and tried to smile. "Can you help me get to Aunt Laura's house?"

He stared down at her, and she sensed his reluctance. She held her breath.

"Well, I guess so," he muttered.

She struggled to stand up, balancing precariously on one foot. He stepped closer and grabbed her arm. His pudgy fingers dug into her flesh. "What are you doing out here alone?" he said into her ear.

Suddenly aware of her own danger, she babbled, "This fog, it's so confusing in the marsh." Hurriedly she added, "It's a good thing you're here. Oh, and I got my sneakers all muddy—Mother's going to be furious with me."

"Huh," he grunted. "Let's get going, then."

It wasn't far to Aunt Laura's house, but to Connie's anxious mind, getting there took forever. Mr. Stafford smelled of stale bacon grease and sweat, and the pain in her ankle worsened with every step.

Her thoughts raced ahead to Dan and Ricky. Where had they gone—and had they managed to catch Tatum? She wondered dizzily if Mr. Stafford suspected that she had overheard their talk. Probably not—or he would have done something dreadful to her by now.

"Connie, what happened?" Mother was standing on the back lawn. The light from the porch was only a fuzzy white blob, but it looked like a welcoming beacon.

"I twisted my ankle again," Connie told her hurriedly. "Mr. Stafford helped me up the hill." How was she going to get him into the house?

Mother beamed at Mr. Stafford. "That was so kind of you!" She took a step closer to them, and Connie stumbled away from Mr. Stafford's grip, half-falling into her arms.

"Get him to come inside," she whispered.

"Oh, Mr. Stafford, you're here at just the right time," Mother said brightly. "We made a coconut cream pie today. Wouldn't you like a piece?"

"Well . . ." The plump man hesitated, and Connie could feel his impatience. Of course he wanted to get away and hide the shell. But his face smoothed into agreeable lines. "I just can't pass up an invitation like that; no, I certainly can't."

Connie sagged with relief. Now he sounded more like his old self. Mother helped her to a chair on the porch. "You'd better get that elastic bandage back onto your ankle," she said. "And look at those shoes of yours!"

"Sorry, I'll take them off right away," Connie mumbled. As she bent over them, she saw that for once Mr. Stafford was taking off his big muddy fishing boots too.

Mother led him into the house, asking questions and chattering about the fog. Connie limped after them. Mother was doing a wonderful job—Dan must have said something to her. But where were Dan and Ricky?

"Sit right here in the living room with Laura," Mother was telling Mr. Stafford. "I'll bring you that pie. Would you like some coffee with it?"

"Yes, please, if it's handy." The smile on his face faded as a police siren wailed through the night.

"Oh, I meant to ask you," said Mother, "did you see anyone suspicious out there? We've had a problem with a prowler tonight. I tried to phone you, but there was no answer, so I called the police."

Mr. Stafford shook his head, looking surprised, and said nothing. He seemed to be listening to the siren, which came closer and closer until it was unbearably loud. Suddenly it shut off.

From the sofa, Aunt Laura spoke calmly. "It's wonderful that the police could get here so fast. They must have been over at the refuge."

She asked Mr. Stafford a question, but Connie didn't wait for his answer. She hobbled to the front door with Mother following. As she opened it, Ricky came running out of the fog-shrouded trees. "We got him!" he cried. "Over here—" He waved frantically.

Two policeman left the car and ran into the woods with him. A moment later they reappeared with Hank, who was dazed-looking and hatless. Behind them came Dan and Ricky, smeared with mud but wearing triumphant grins.

Mother opened the door wide. "Come in, everybody," she exclaimed, and she led them into the living room.

Aunt Laura was saying, "But Ben, you haven't had your pie yet." She greeted the tall, grey-haired policeman who seemed to be in charge. "Hello, Tom."

"Good to see you up and around, Laura," he said politely. "Heard you've got a problem with prowlers."

Connie held her breath as Aunt Laura sat forward and peered at the man who called himself Hank. "Why Hank Tatum, I do believe it's you—without your mustache," she said. "What are you doing back here?"

He ignored her question. "Tell these kids they made a mistake," he said stiffly.

"Aunt Laura, we're pretty sure he's the one who's been trying to break into your house," Connie put in.

Tom Frost looked interested. "Laura, have you met this man before?"

"Yes," she said quietly, "he used to work for us. Then my husband fired him."

"Do you know why?"

Aunt Laura gazed sadly at Hank Tatum. "Philip thought he was stealing from the shell collection."

"Hey!" Ricky exclaimed. "Maybe all those shells over at Hank's house aren't his."

"Wait a minute," interrupted Hank. "Lots of people have shell collections." He glared at Ricky. "And the say-so of some little ragamuffin is no kind of proof."

Aunt Laura spoke quietly to Tom Frost. "I think we can find out if there's any truth to it. My husband was very careful about identifying his shells."

Connie had a sudden idea. "Ricky, do you still have the shell that Coon took from the cabin?"

His muddy face lit up. "Yup. Got a secret pocket here." He fished deep in the torn lining of his jacket and pulled it out.

Aunt Laura turned the small striped shell over in her hand. "It's an Elliot's volute," she murmured. "There's only one way to be sure that it belonged to Philip."

She glanced at Dan. "We have an ultraviolet lamp in the shell room upstairs. Do you know what one looks like?"

"Sure." Dan's eyes shone with what Connie called his 'scientific gleam of interest.'

"Try looking in one of those deep drawers," Aunt Laura told him. "It may have been disassembled."

"Okay. C'mon, Rick." The two boys pounded up the stairs.

"We'll need an extension cord too, I think," Aunt Laura went on.

"There's one in the kitchen. I'll get it," Mother said.

Connie examined the striped volute curiously. It didn't seem to have a mark on it.

Chapter Twenty
The Answer

By the time Mother returned and they had cleared a space on the coffee table, the boys were back. Ricky carried in something that looked like the base for a sun lamp, and Dan held a large light bulb that reminded Connie of a floodlight.

He screwed the light bulb into its base and turned it on. It had an odd, purplish glow. "That's ultraviolet," he remarked with a grin of satisfaction.

"It works better in the dark," Aunt Laura said. "Philip numbered all of his volutes in the seventies," she added.

Mother turned off the living room lights, and Dan moved the ultraviolet lamp so that it shone on the shell. A tiny number glowed with bright white intensity on the pale shell. Dan bent over it. "Looks like *73*," he exclaimed. "He must have put it on with some kind of fluorescent ink."

Tom Frost leaned over to take a look and nodded.

Dan switched off the ultraviolet lamp and turned on the living room lights. Connie watched Hank Tatum closely. He was chewing on his lip as if he were trying to think what to say next.

Mr. Stafford, who had been remarkably quiet all this time, got to his feet and smiled at Aunt Laura. "Well, I guess that settles it. I'll be getting along, Laura. Let me know if you need anything." Hank Tatum jerked around to face him. "Oh, no you don't," he muttered. "You're not leaving me holdin' the bag."

The surprised look on Aunt Laura's face made Connie speak up. "We heard Hank give the golden cowrie to Mr. Stafford tonight. Hank must have been working for him."

Mr. Stafford smiled benignly, as though he were humoring a child's foolishness. "That's ridiculous. Go ahead and search me."

Connie's heart sank. He sounded so sure of himself. But he wouldn't have had time to hide it anywhere, would he?—unless he just dropped it under a bush outside. What had he done with that shell?

She stared at him, thinking hard, and her gaze rested on his stockinged feet. His boots! His big fishing boots that he never took off—not until tonight. . . .

While Tom Frost checked through Mr. Stafford's pockets, she limped over to the policeman by the door and quietly explained. He nodded and disappeared. A minute later he carried Mr. Stafford's fishing boots into the living room. He put them down on the carpet with an apologetic look at Aunt Laura.

Tom Frost had finished searching Mr. Stafford. He gave Connie a quick glance. "Think it might be in those boots?"

Connie didn't trust her voice to answer. She nodded.

Mr. Stafford made a gesture of protest, and the policeman looked at him. "With your permission, sir?"

Mr. Stafford shrugged and sat down.

Connie leaned forward to watch. Tom Frost put his hand into the depths of each boot and came up empty. Then he tried the zippered side compartments. From the second one he pulled out a shining golden shell, and Connie sank back against the sofa cushions.

The policeman handed it to Aunt Laura. "Oh, I never thought I'd see our golden cowrie again," she exclaimed. Then her face shadowed and she turned to Mr. Stafford with a questioning look.

Mr. Stafford eyed Hank Tatum. His face had lost some of its pink color, but his voice rolled out deep and unconcerned. "Now, boy, why did you put that shell into my boot? You trying to get me into trouble? Huh?"

He glanced at Aunt Laura. "I'm not sure I even know this man. Why would he do a thing like that?"

Hank Tatum's dark eyes flashed. "You old geezer, you got me into this! You're the one who wanted the shell in the first place. And you started the burglary rumors, and you even staged the break-in at your own house."

Mr. Stafford cut him off with an impatient gesture. "That's a mighty peculiar tale you're telling. I never did arrange anything with you."

Ricky burst out indignantly. "Aw, he's lying. We heard them two talking together just tonight."

Dan gave Connie a swift glance. "And didn't we see them together when we were up in the airplane with Stella?"

Tom Frost stepped forward. "Well, I think there's enough evidence here to warrant an investigation. We'll take these two gentlemen on down to the station and find out what they have to say for themselves."

"Tatum," Aunt Laura said quietly, "just tell me, were you the one who broke into the house—that time during the storm?"

Hank Tatum looked worried now. Slowly he nodded. "Yes, I wanted to get the diary that told where your husband had put the golden cowrie. I'd hidden the diary behind some books in his library so I could go back and finish reading it. Since the electricity was off in the whole neighborhood, I thought it would be easy to just grab it and run."

He gave her a pleading glance. "I'm sorry you fell down those stairs—I didn't mean to brush so close when I ran past you—I guess I made you lose your balance—"

"I don't believe it. I think he pushed you," interrupted Mr. Stafford. His voice shook with rage. "He's just a lying, no-good, thieving—"

"All right, that's enough," ordered Tom Frost. "Let's get going."

After the men had gone, Mother exclaimed, "Look how late it is! You youngsters must be starved." She smiled at Ricky. "I'll phone your parents and ask if you can stay for supper—then I'll drive you home. Would you like that?"

Ricky shrugged. "Sounds okay. You don't have to phone, though. My dad won't be home 'til after midnight and he don't care anyhow."

Mother looked a little startled, but she said, "Well, I'll see about supper." A minute later she was back with an ice pack and the elastic bandage. She handed them to Connie. "You'd better get this ice on your ankle right away."

"Okay." Connie eased herself down onto the carpet with a sigh.

"Hey, Ricky," Dan said, "want to come up to my room for a while?"

"Sure," Ricky said, and Connie was glad to hear the eagerness in his voice.

When they were alone, Aunt Laura gazed for a minute at the golden cowrie, still clasped in her hands, then she said softly, "Connie, it happened today."

Connie looked up from the icebag on her ankle. "What happened?"

Aunt Laura's blue eyes were dancing. "The Lord gave us the rest of His answer."

"What? How?" exclaimed Connie. "Tell me everything!"

Aunt Laura rested her head against the back of the sofa and smiled. "This afternoon when you were outside, a man named Jason Ross stopped by."

"From the museum!"

Aunt Laura nodded serenely. "He came to ask about the golden cowrie. I told him that it wasn't for sale, and while we were talking, he said he'd like to see the rest of Philip's collection. Your mother took him up to the study, and he spent a long time looking over the shells. He wants to buy Philip's whole set of cowries. Apparently we have one, a brown-toothed cowrie, that's even more rare than the golden."

"The whole set?" Connie said in wonder. "Will he pay enough?"

Aunt Laura's dimples deepened. "Just enough."

"Oh, that's great!" Connie started to jump up and remembered her ankle just in time. Happily she tossed the ice pack into the air.

Aunt Laura said, "I can't thank you enough for getting our golden cowrie back."

Connie picked up one end of the elastic bandage and started winding it around her foot before she answered. "I had this great idea of finding that shell so you could sell it and get the money for your house," she said soberly. "Then I discovered that your husband didn't want to sell it, and I was really discouraged. I couldn't see how you'd ever get the money."

She went on to tell Aunt Laura all about finding the shell in the birdhouse. Then she had to smile, just thinking about it. "I was so worried, but the Lord had everything planned and it turned out perfectly."

"Yes, it really did," Aunt Laura agreed. "It's marvelous—everything that's happened since He brought you all here—and now I'm getting better, too."

"Stella will be glad, won't she?" said Connie. "I'm going to write her about it, and Mother said we could ask her to come and visit us."

Her mother called from the kitchen, "Connie, I could use some help, if your ankle's not too bad."

"Sure, almost done." Connie finished bandaging her ankle and stood up to test it. She limped slowly toward the kitchen and found that Aunt Laura was following her. "Aren't you supposed to rest or something?" she asked her aunt.

"Nope," Aunt Laura said, "I'm coming out to help too."

After they had eaten, Mother took Ricky home. While she was gone, Connie and Dan finished cleaning up the kitchen. Connie told him how Ricky had been hired by Tatum and then had changed his mind. "That reminds me," she exclaimed. "When we were talking, Ricky said something wonderful—I meant to tell you before—it sounds as if the Lord is really working in his heart. He said he needs to talk to you again."

Dan stopped drying the plate in his hand. "After what happened, I almost gave up on him," he said slowly. "I'd about decided that the only person he'd ever listen to was you."

"Me?"

"Yes, you've made a friend out of him, somehow." Dan paused, the way he did when he was thinking things through. "You did it with Aunt Laura, too. Maybe caring about people—making friends with them—is a special talent. Anyway, I think you've got it. I sure wish I did."

Connie was so surprised that she couldn't think of anything to say. She scrubbed hard at an already-clean bowl, and warm happiness spread inside her.

Dan added, "I sort of wondered if something had happened to Ricky. Tonight, up in my room, he was asking a bunch of questions about the Bible. He's coming back over tomorrow, so I'll make sure I have some answers ready."

He grinned at Connie. "It's all because of you, sis."

For some reason, Connie didn't mind the nickname when he said it like that. She let out the dishwater and leaned against the sink with a contented sigh. "It's because of the Lord, you mean. Just think—the shell is safe, Ricky might get saved, and Aunt Laura can give her house to the mission."

She flipped a dishtowel at him and grinned. "When Aunt Mabel gets here tomorrow, there won't be anything left for her to organize. The Lord's done it all."